THE THROWBACK

David Canford

Mad-books.com

To Ann

Cover Design By: Mary Ann Dujardin

Cover Photo: Ashely Knedler

SIGN UP TO RECEIVE DAVID CANFORD'S EMAIL NEWSLETTER AT DAVIDCANFORD.COM INCLUDING INFORMATION ON NEW BOOK RELEASES AND PROMOTIONS AND CLAIM YOUR FREE EBOOK

CHAPTER 1

Her screams reverberated throughout the house.

"Take that boy outside," shouted George Elwood at the young black woman whose hand the child was tightly clinging to with his own, his face a mixture of fright and bewilderment.

The man retreated to his study. Shaking, he poured himself a glass of bourbon. His hand stuck to the bottle. It wasn't a particularly hot day but he was sweating profusely. So much depended on this birth. The future of his family, the very future of the plantation itself.

As he raised the glass to his lips, the screaming stopped. His mouth became dry and his heart missed a beat. There was silence. Had she...?

A baby's cry rang out. George's shoulders subsided in relief. The baby hadn't died and hopefully neither had his wife, although the well being of the child was by far his greater concern. He tore across the hall and up the curved staircase. The doctor had emerged from the bedroom in his shirt sleeves, his brow furrowed.

"Mr. Elwood, there's something-"

But George had either not heard, or had chosen to

ignore him. His wife lay half propped up in bed. Her complexion was pallid. She said nothing but her look was one of exhaustion. Maisie, the nurse-maid, was seated on a chair cradling the child. George stormed over eagerly.

"Give him to me." That the child might be a girl, he didn't want to even contemplate.

Maisie's eyes were wide open with fear as if she had been cornered by a predator.

"Now," he commanded.

She tentatively raised the small, blanketed bundle toward him. He grabbed it impatiently. The smile forming on his lips was extinguished in an instant.

"What in God's name!"

Maisie had already stood, retreating against the wall as though hoping that it might open up and swallow her whole. She was only a small person, under five feet in height. Her large eyes seemed too big for her face. There wasn't an ounce of fat on her. Like most other slaves, she was thin from a life of physical labor and barely getting enough to eat. George, while not particularly tall, towered above her, the buttons on his shirt straining against his stomach made round from a life of good food and drink. He threw the baby back at her, his expression displaying utter disgust.

"What kind of sick joke is this? I'll have you whipped. Where is my child?"

The doctor was beside him now.

"She is your wife's child. She's had a...girl."

"You mean my wife's a whore, a nigger's whore.

That baby is brown."

George went across to the bed, his face puce with rage.

"Well?" he demanded.

"She's ours, George. I swear. I have never been with anyone but you."

"You're lying. How could you betray me like this."

"Mr. Elwood, sir," interrupted the doctor. "I have heard of very rare cases where a color from an ancestor can unexpectedly resurface in later generations."

"Well, there's no such ancestor in my family. Did you lie to me about your heritage, Jane? Is that why your hair and eyes are so dark, and you tan in the slightest of sun?"

"Of course not."

This child was a monumental disgrace. Some of his female slaves had borne children of his. That was accepted. Expected even. There was no shame in that. Many plantation wives welcomed it. It lessened the demands on them, and fewer children meant less likelihood of dying in childbirth. It also made good business sense, using those who were considered as assets not persons to produce more. But if word ever got out that his wife had given birth to a mixed race baby that would create lifelong ignominy for him and the family name.

George was convinced that his wife was lying. She must have laid with a male slave. How else could this have happened? The affection he felt for Jane, which had already waned considerably since their marriage over five years ago, was no more. His wife had become repulsive to him.

The man's mind raced. He must act quickly and decisively before word could get out.

"I can trust you never to utter a word about this, Doctor?"

"Of course, patient confidentiality demands it."

"Good. You can go now. Send me your bill. And close the door behind you."

The two women in the room looked terrified. Although only one was a slave, George held complete power over both of them.

He advanced toward Maisie to take the child. Her life needed to be ended immediately. Both women sensed his intention. Tears coursed freely down Maisie's cheeks.

"No, George," pleaded his wife.

He hesitated. Each of the women exhaled. It seemed that there was hope.

"Maisie, after dark tonight you will take this thing and drown her. Let her body float down the river. No one will give it a second thought if she should be washed up. They'll merely conclude a nigger girl has misbehaved. You will ensure no one sees you, and that you never say a single word about this. If you fail me, I will give you the whipping of your life, and sell you away from Nathaniel and your children. Do you understand me?"

"Yes, Mas'r," she said, keeping her head down. Maisie had always known you never looked white folk directly in the eye. It made them mad, could get you a beating.

"You may look at me. Look at me and promise me." She slowly raised her head. "Promise me, damn you woman."

"I promise."

"You will both wait here until I return. Keep the drapes closed."

George locked the door as he left and took the key, leaving them in semi-darkness. A thin arrow of the bright day outside pierced the narrow space between the two crimson drapes, creating a line of light across the room which climbed up the opposite wall.

The two women were in shock as they had been from the moment when they had seen the child emerge from her mother. Maisie said nothing. She had to live a life where she wasn't supposed to speak unless spoken to. She held the child close for the baby's comfort and her own. None of this was her doing but she would pay the price if anything went wrong.

Jane turned her head away from Maisie. She felt such shame. Color was the absolute arbiter here in South Carolina. White and you could be respectable if you adhered to the societal requirements to be so. Reputation meant everything. Lose that and you would be shunned. The rules were black and white, there was no gray. Not one drop was allowed. One drop of African blood and you weren't regarded as white or respectable. Produce a brown baby and your name would be dirt. Your friends would ignore you. They had no choice in the matter. If they didn't, they too would be cast out from what passed for polite society.

Although Jane would never have been able to acknowledge this defenseless little creature as her daughter, killing the baby seemed wrong. She could be looked after by their slaves or given to another plantation if that were deemed unacceptable by her husband. Yet his rage and her horror at having produced a child who wasn't white had robbed her of the will to make any effort to change his mind.

The girl began to wriggle. Maisie knew she would soon cry, so she pulled down the top of her frayed dress to expose her breast and let the baby suckle. That was to have been Maisie's job. She had been taken from her one room shack to be the child's milk cow to ensure that her real mother wouldn't be inconvenienced by nature's demands. Maisie's youngest was ready to be weaned and she was now to live in the big house apart from her family. Her heart was heavy with sadness at that separation, but how she felt didn't count for anything in this world. Her wishes were of no consequence. They had to remain unsaid at all times.

When dusk arrived, George Elwood returned. Both women sat up straight and rigid as they heard his footsteps ascending the stairs, ominous like the approach of an executioner. The key turned in the lock. Their jailor stood there showing no hint of pity or remorse.

"You can take her now, Maisie. Remember what I said."

Silently and looking down at the floor, she left the room carrying her human parcel, the baby's face covered by the blanket. Small bumps appeared along its surface as the little girl inside moved her limbs. Maisie's embrace must have felt warm and reassuring. The baby would have had no idea of the fate that awaited her.

George pulled back a drape to watch Maisie exit from the back of the house and make her way in the direction of the river and merge into the fast fading light. That part of the problem was at least dealt with. He turned.

"Get up." His voice remained as sharp as broken glass.

"But George, I can hardly stand."

"Well, you're going to have to."

"No."

Enraged by her defiance, he slapped his wife across the face and pulled back her bedclothes.

"You'll do as I say. You've caused me more than enough trouble already."

Jane fell toward him as she got up. He put out his hands to steady her, holding her at arms' length as if she was something that smelled unpleasant. After a moment, he let go.

"Where are you taking me? And what about Thomas?"

"Somewhere where the disgrace you have brought on this family will be kept out of the public eye."

"You can't do this."

"I can do what the hell I want. Thank your lucky stars that I don't go get my gun and shoot you. If you don't co-operate with me, you'll never see your son again."

Jane's legs gave way and she fell to the floor. George grabbed her under the arms from behind and dragged her backward out of the bedroom as though she was already a corpse. She was in no fit state to travel and might die on the journey. However, he no longer cared. That outcome would suit him best of all.

"Jeremiah, come help me."

A man came running up the stairs.

"My wife needs to get to the hospital in town. Help me carry her."

Maneuvring a body too tired to resist down the staircase and the steps leading from the front door, they carried her into the carriage outside.

"Do you want me to drive, Mas'r?"

"No, I'll go alone."

George jumped up onto the driver's seat and hit the horse's rear end with his riding crop.

Jeremiah lifted his bowed head and watched them disappear into the night. If the truth be told he wasn't sorry to see her go and wouldn't care if she never returned.

CHAPTER 2

Maisie hurried through the long grass, panting from the exertion. She wasn't used to walking so fast, the South Carolina climate was too hot for that.

Crickets chirped and in the distance she could hear singing from the slave quarters, an uplifting cappella which refused to succumb to the harshness of their daily life. Those voices helped soothe her after the trauma that had been today. It was the sound of home. Her home. The only home that she had ever known. The only one which she ever would, should her daily prayers that she and her family remain here together and not be sold off separately be answered.

She and Nathaniel owned no material things. They couldn't even get married in the eyes of the law, just jump over the broom. But they had each other, and they had their family. That meant everything to her.

Maisie wondered if her children were now sleeping. How she wished she could be there to kiss them goodnight. At least she should be reunited with them soon. There would be no baby to care for now.

Up ahead she saw it. Black even in the moonlight, like a huge snake slithering this way and that. Maisie didn't like rivers. They were invisible fences, another hazard if you tried to run. She couldn't swim. The water frightened her and she knew this one could be deep.

Maisie crouched down by the river's edge, placing her human package on the ground. All she had to do was shove it. Roll it off the bank and be done. In an instant, it would all be over.

The child may be brown, but she had come from the white people who enslaved her and her family. Why should she care? But Maisie did care. She was a mother. A source of life, not death. She opened the blanket and looked at that little face, those tiny hands. A helpless creature.

Maisie's dilemma was harrowing. If she saved the child, she could lose her family and never see them again. If she threw the baby into the river, she would be a murderer. Why her, why did she have to be the one caught up in all this? Maisie sank onto her rear and wept.

Crying cleared her mind. Wrapping the blanket back around the child, she picked her up and walked toward a path that would take her to the adjacent plantation. The entire time she scanned the shadows, ready to jump into the forest should she see anyone approaching.

Being out here at night was forbidden. George Elwood could get to hear of it, and worse than that, get to hear that she still had the baby with her. She was tempted to run back to the river and be done with it. All the while she battled her nerves, and at times they almost won.

Maisie reached a group of flimsy wooden huts. She knew the one that she wanted. The one where her friend lived. Maisie had been allowed to visit her before, after Ella had been sold to Gregory Brown by George Elwood a few years back. She pushed on the door and went in. There were five sleeping. Two adults and a baby on a crude wooden bed, and two children on another. Maisie gently touched Ella's arm.

"Maisie?" she whispered in surprise.

"Come outside."

Ella followed her, wiping the sleep from her eyes.

"What are you doing here? And what's that you got there?"

"What do you think I got?"

"Well, I can see you've got a baby."

"A brown baby, the Masr's."

"Yours?"

"Lord, no. He wanted me to drown her in the river but I couldn't. Poor child ain't never hurt no one. I was hoping you might find someone here who could feed her and look after her. I'm sure your Mas'r would be happy enough when he found there was another child he could work when she gets older."

"Oh my. I don't know what to say."

"Say yes or I gotta kill her and I can't do that."

"I understand but-"

"Please Ella."

"You're right. If we go around killing children, we ain't no better than them that keep us here against our will. I'll find someone. What's she called?"

"I hadn't thought… Mosa. Mosa, that's her name."

"Mosa?"

"Yeah, after Moses, hidden in the bullrushes so the Pharaoh couldn't kill him."

"Mosa it is then."

"I better feed her one more time before I go."

As Maisie let her suckle, they swopped news of their families.

"Good luck little one," she said as she handed the baby over. "I must be going. Get on back before he starts to wonder where I am. Thank you Ella, you're a true friend. And remember, never mention where she came from."

"I won't. You take care of yourself."

Maisie returned the way which she had come. She should have felt unburdened but she didn't. A dark thought crossed her mind like the cloud now blocking out the moon above. What if George Elwood hadn't been telling the truth or changed his mind? What if he sold her anyway to make sure that she was out of the way to be certain word never got out. Involuntarily, she let out a cry of anguish at the thought that she would then never see her family again.

CHAPTER 3

Maisie knocked gently on the door.

"Come in."

She worried that the noise of her racing heartbeat must be audible to him.

"You sent for me, Mas'r?"

"Yes. Shut the door."

She felt such stress, as though it had solid form and was standing next to George Elwood. As if it knew the truth and would whisper it into his ear.

The man had dark circles under his eyes. He must have slept badly like her. His clothes were creased and appeared to be the same as he was wearing yesterday. His hostile demeanor was also little changed.

"You did what I asked?"

"Yes, Mas'r."

"Look at me when I ask you a question."

He got up from his chair and came over, peering into her eyes. Her legs began to tremble and Maisie gave thanks that they were covered by the coarse brown material which was her dress. Her only dress. She clasped her hands together so that he wouldn't notice them shaking.

"Hmm."

His utterance was non-committal. She prayed silently that she wasn't to be sold.

He turned and walked away, saying nothing for a while. It may only have been a few seconds but to Maisie it felt an eternity.

"You're not needed here anymore."

Maisie fought to stay standing. She wanted to sink to the ground and beg, but she knew that would be pointless.

Maisie had witnessed it before, when others had pleaded to remain here with their family. Elwood didn't regard their feelings as relevant, probably didn't even regard them as capable of true emotions. To him they were little different than his livestock, his property to use and dispose of as he saw fit. He showed affection to his horses, but not his human creatures, except for the young women who satisfied him. And that wasn't real affection which he displayed, just post coital contentment which mellowed him for a short while. He had been raised to believe that slaves were somewhere between ape and human, and could be treated accordingly.

"You are to return to work in the fields."

She wanted to say "Yes, Mas'r" as she knew she should, but her relief choked off her voice.

"Be gone then."

Maisie hurried from the house, almost unable to believe her good luck, if any part of her existence could be viewed as such. She wanted to jump with joy. She was going back to be with her family. Yes, she would work from morning until night, her every limb aching from her toil. But they would all be staying together for now at least. Maisie tried not to think too far into the future, because she had no power to alter it, and that thought frightened her.

Her young children were playing in the dirt. When they saw her, they ran to her and she got down to embrace them, their hugs a comfort after what she had endured these past twenty-four hours.

In the evening, Nathaniel returned. His face creased into a big smile when he saw his wife.

"How come you're here? Did they let you come see us?"

"The baby died," she lied. "They don't need me in the house no more."

"And Miss Elwood?"

"Jeremiah just told me she gone died too. Elwood took her to the hospital in town. She was dead on arrival. He shouldn't have moved her. She was too weak for the journey."

Nathaniel expressed no opinion. What happened to the mistress shouldn't affect them. The death of the master was what he feared. If he died then whoever took control, that could change their lives. Elwood was no avuncular figure, but there were worse masters than him. Whippings here were infrequent. Yes, runaways were treated harshly. They all knew that if you made a bolt for freedom you sure better not catch you. There were better places to be, but many much worse.

CHAPTER 4

Clarrisa Elwood sighed with irritation when she received the news. She had been looking forward to a night at the theater in Charleston. She had moved back to the city after her husband's death. There were things to entertain her here, unlike the genteel claustrophobia which was so often a white woman's lot on a plantation.

Her daughter-in-law's death didn't sadden her. Clarissa had never really liked Jane. Her son could have done so much better, have married someone with the prospect of a much bigger inheritance, or at least a better social standing.

She put her grandson's inadequate physical condition down to Jane's genes. The Elwoods had always been strong and healthy. That withered leg which Thomas dragged behind him was a badge of shame for the family. How could a boy like that take over the plantation when his father passed on. A suitable heir was still needed

In public Clarissa would show some grief for appearance's sake, but death in childbirth and infant mortality weren't unexpected events. Best to look at it as an opportunity was her opinion.

On this occasion, death had a silver lining. George could remarry and Clarissa could have a hand in ensuring that he didn't make a poor choice this time.

When her carriage arrived at the large white-painted mansion with its wrap around verandas the following afternoon, her son helped her down. Her grandson stood by the front door holding a maid's hand as he sniveled, grieving the loss of his mother.

"You must learn to be a man, Thomas, like your father."

It was her only greeting as she passed him to enter the house.

After dinner, Clarissa and her son sat in the drawing room, a large portrait of her husband, his father, above them.

"What was the child?"

"A girl."

"Well, at least you didn't lose a son."

George swirled his glass of whisky, watching it intently.

"What are you hiding from me, George?"

"Nothing."

"Don't lie to me. You forget, I'm your mother. I can tell when something's bothering you."

"Leave us and go to bed," snapped George at Jeremiah who was standing by the wall, forced to wait still and silent for hours in case George or his mother should demand something.

George looked over his shoulder to check the door

had closed behind the man.

"The child was an abomination."

"In that case, we should thank the Lord that he saw fit to take her. This family doesn't need another cripple that's for sure."

"She wasn't deformed."

"What was wrong with her then?"

He opened his mouth but no words would come.

"George? Answer my question."

"She...she was...My wife betrayed me. The child was brown."

Contrary to what he had expected, his mother's mouth didn't fall open with shock. She remained perfectly calm.

"You think it wasn't yours?"

"Obviously. She must have had carnal relations with a negro. Why are you not disgusted? It is so shameful."

"George, there's something you don't know about our family." She had lowered her voice to a whisper. "Your great grandmother... she wasn't white." He sat up in his chair, gripping the arms of it as if a bolt of lightning had shot right through him.

"What?"

"She was a mulatto, mixed race. Though by all accounts it hardly showed. Her mother was born in England. It seems she fell madly in love with a free African. She knew their union would never be allowed by her family so they came to America where Grace, my grandmother, was born.

"They found a place in Boston but their relationship didn't last. It couldn't. Grace grew up in poverty, but her beauty saved her. A young man up there on business from Charleston met her and fell for her. That was your great grandfather. They had my mother. She survived but Grace died shortly after the birth. My grandfather brought my mother down here when his business in New York failed. My mother, as you may recall, was as white as snow."

"So what the doctor said, about it being possible that the color of the child was caused by a throwback to our ancestors, was correct?"

"Yes. There were many things about Jane that weren't to my taste, but a woman of loose morals was something which I believe she most certainly wasn't."

George bit his lip as he absorbed the news and its ramifications.

"Did father know?"

"No, I had no reason to tell him."

"Why tell me then?"

"Because I could see at dinner you were traumatized. I put it down to Jane's passing, but when you told me about the child I understood it was worse than that, that you were tortured by the thought of what you believed your wife had done to you. It's over, George. Such things don't happen twice. The child is dead. Jane is dead. Let's speak of this no more. I want you to find happiness and have an heir capable of carrying my late husband's legacy into the future."

Next morning, as commanded by the overseer, the slaves stood in two lines, heads bowed as pallbearers lifted two coffins, one large and one small, out of the mourning carriage.

Waiting there, Maisie felt that fear return. Only two people here knew that one coffin was empty. She and George Elwood. How she wished she didn't know. Her secret weighed upon her daily, like a parrot whose claws dug into her shoulder, threatening to shout it out loud. It was a truth she would much have preferred not to know, but it was one which she could never escape from. A secret that threatened to unravel her life at any moment.

George, his mother, and Thomas led the procession behind the coffins. Friends followed them into the small family graveyard near the house where the priest presided over the burial.

Thomas reached for his father's hand. The man flicked it away as though getting rid of an annoying fly.

CHAPTER 5

Thomas wondered what he had done wrong when he was told that his father wished to see him downstairs. And worse, what the punishment would be.

Thomas lived largely out of sight, in the black world. He preferred that. They smiled at him, they laughed often. Most of them actually seemed to like him. He didn't believe his father did. Even less so after his mother and sister had died. A sister who he had never seen.

Since his mother's death, Thomas had spent barely any time with his father, although he had rarely got to spend much time with him before.

He missed his mother, sitting on her lap and smelling her perfume whilst sinking into the voluminous material of her dress. Not that he had seen her more than once or twice a day.

Jemima, who had looked after him since he was a baby, was generous with her hugs but only in private. They both understood that in his father's world there was a division which had to be maintained.

Thomas usually ate in the kitchen. Meal times at

the family table were an arduous affair, requiring him to stay silent and eat everything on his plate, even the food he hated.

His only playmates had been some of the young slave children. But now five years old, they were required to take water out to the adults in the fields and run other errands. For him, an education would soon begin.

"Enter," called his father in response to his son's knock. The tone was cold and formal.

Jemima pushed a reluctant Thomas into the room and waited outside.

"Thomas, I would like you to meet Emma."

A smiling lady with her blond hair in ringlets and a yellow dress standing next to his father, bent down a little and put her hands out in greeting.

"Hello, Thomas. I'm very happy to make your acquaintance."

Thomas had frozen like a statue.

"He's a pitifully shy boy," said his father with disdain. "Thomas, I have some wonderful news. Emma is to be your new mother."

She bent forward again.

"You may hug me."

This time Thomas moved in, briefly putting his arms around the folds of her dress while she tussled his hair. It was an awkward encounter.

"You may go now," said his father.

George found even less to like in the boy these days. He was the image of his mother with his curly chestnut hair and large hazel colored eyes that seemed to plead for compromise, not a determination to dominate as did his father's.

Thomas exited quickly into the warm embrace of Jemima.

"I'm getting a new mother. Her name's Emma."

His voice was flat as if he were relaying the day's shopping list.

"Why, that's wonderful news."

"I wish I was your color."

"Whatever for?"

"So I could live in the slave quarters."

"Why would you wish such a thing when you live in this beautiful house?"

"Because I don't like it. You won't ever leave me, will you?"

"Not if I have anything to do with it," Jemima reassured him though she knew she would have no say in the matter. "Come, let's go to the kitchen and see what cook can give you."

Thomas found the wedding a boring affair. His new trousers itched terribly and his shirt was tight around the neck. He thought of his friends back at the plantation, charging around in the dirt. It wasn't fair that he had to sit silently in this gloomy church.

Nice things didn't happen here. Less than a year ago, he had sat in the exact same spot for his mother's funeral under orders to keep quiet and absolutely still, just like today.

After what seemed an age, it was over. He had to ride in a carriage with his grandmother. She must surely be a witch thought Thomas, dressed all in black with a black bonnet and black lace fingerless gloves covering her hands. He had never seen her in any other color.

"Whatever are you looking so glum for, boy?" she snapped. "You have a new mother to look after you now. Hopefully, someone who'll stop you running around out of control like a pickaninny. It's about time you learned your place in society. You were fortunate to be born into a highly respected family, and it is your duty to live up to the Elwood name."

Thomas hoped his new mother would just leave him be.

Back at the house, a long table had been laid outside under a large canopy in the bright sunshine. If the table were animate it surely would have groaned under the weight of food piled upon it.

His mood rose as he took in the happy atmosphere and observed his cousins playing. His father even smiled at him.

"You may go play with them, but don't get your clothes dirty."

Thomas limped across the grass to join the three boys and one girl.

"What do you want?" demanded the eldest boy.

"My father said I could come and play with you."

"Play? How can you. You can't run. Go away."

Thomas wanted to cry but he couldn't let them see that he was upset so he turned and went in the direction of the slave quarters. They at least wouldn't reject him.

To mark the celebration, the slaves had been given a rare day off, and his father had allowed them to kill a hog to roast. They were in high spirits.

"Do you want some meat?" asked Nathaniel.

Thomas nodded. Maisie put some in a wooden bowl and beckoned him to come sit on the ground with them.

"Mom, can we go now?" asked one of her brood.

"You all ate your food?" They nodded. "Good. Well, I guess you can."

She noticed Thomas watching them run off.

"Ain't you hungry?"

He shook his head.

"I suppose this ain't no treat for you. Y'all get meat every single day up in the big house. You can go join them."

"Poor kid," she said as he shuffled slowly off.

"Poor kid? You gotta be kidding me," said her husband. "A full belly every day, a life of luxury, and you call him poor? Our babies ain't ever gonna have even a tiny piece of what he has."

"That sure is true but I don't think he's loved, and that's a terrible thing."

"You're too damn soft woman."

George Elwood wasn't and gave his son a beating when he returned home with his clothes soiled with mud.

CHAPTER 6

A few years later Mosa had reached the age of seven. She too hadn't experienced parental love.

Eliza, the woman who had taken her in, had recently lost her first baby but she had since produced three of her own. Agreeing to look after Mosa had seemed a good idea at the time. It didn't now. Eliza's hands were full and her man had been sold last winter, sent to the slave market in Charleston.

He'd ended up in Mississippi they said. She would never see him again or the children their father. She didn't know where he was, and he would doubtless be known by his new owner's name. Anyway she couldn't write. It was worse than living with the certainty of death. That brought closure. Knowing that a loved one was still alive but you could never see them as long as they lived, not even know if they were all right, was a torment which didn't lessen with the passing of time.

Mosa was of little use around the place, more a hindrance than a help. She broke things and burned the cooking. Eliza considered that she had a haughty attitude, as though she was born above it all. It must be due to her father's blood, Eliza reasoned. These half and halves sensed they were different from an early age. In Eliza's opinion, most carried resentment on their faces plain for all to see. Some got jobs in the house if their fathers had a conscience, and their wives would allow it. But Mosa was unlikely to escape a life in the fields. Her father was apparently from another plantation.

Mosa was probably still too young to know why she might feel as though there had been a mistake, that she shouldn't be here. As she grew older, that vague feeling would develop into something tangible, something Eliza would have to try beating out of her. Eliza was quite convinced of it.

Yet Mosa's concern was not how she lived but why she was different. She wished that she was blacker, like the others her age who she lived with. The kids often taunted her.

"You can't play with us, you're not one of us. Mama says your daddy must've been white, but he didn't want you. And we don't either."

Like Thomas, Mosa also soon learned not to cry in front of other children. It only encouraged them to tease her more. She didn't tell Eliza. Eliza only ever scolded her if she tried to confide in her. Instead, Mosa ran off into the forest where she could cry alone.

"You all right, honey?"

Mosa looked up to see a young woman who looked like her, brown not black, brown not white.

"No one will play with me."

"I will. Come on, chase me."

Mosa ran after her. The woman let Mosa catch her, and then it was Mosa's turn. She swung Mosa around when she caught her, causing giggles of delight to erupt from the girl. As she put her down, Mosa staggered unsteadily backward.

"I ain't never seen you before," said Mosa after she had regained her balance.

"That's because I'm new here. Mas'r Gregory bought me last week to work in the house. I should take you back to your Mama."

"I don't have one. Eliza lets me live with her family, but she always tells me I'm not one of her children."

"Oh. My name's Poppy. What's yours?"

"Mosa."

"My, that's a pretty name. Bet-"

"Poppy where are you?"

The voice was gruff and impatient and Poppy's smile evaporated.

"Coming Mas'r. See you again, Mosa. I gotta go now."

She gave her a weak smile as she departed. Mosa watched her run toward Gregory Brown. The man frightened Mosa, not that she had ever spent any time with him but everyone would warn you, annoy him and he'll take a swipe at you if you're lucky, the whip if you're not.

"I told you to wait for me behind the stables. When I tell you where to be, you damn sure better be there in future. Come, we need to be quick."

He must have sensed Mosa looking. Turning his head in her direction, he scowled at her.

"Get outta here."

Mosa departed as fast as her legs would carry her.

CHAPTER 7

"Now you're sixteen, Thomas, you've had more than enough schooling."

"Yes, sir."

Thomas didn't agree but he knew better then to contradict his father. He was standing beside his father's desk. The man would never ask him to sit down.

"It's time you learned practical things, got your nose out of books. Those are for women. It's also time for you to appreciate the gulf between us and the niggers. I don't want to see you out there smiling at them any longer, or hearing reports of you down at the slave quarters passing the time of day in their company. I should've sold Jemima sooner than I did. She corrupted your mind. Made you weak."

Thomas thought of dear Jemima who had taught him to be kind and respectful, who had shown him more love than any of his relatives. He still missed her even though she had been gone for over five years.

"Today, you're gonna learn how to make them respect you," continued his father. "They're like dogs. If you don't show them who's boss, they'll try and take over. Do you understand?"

Thomas failed to respond.

"Answer me boy if you don't want to feel the back of my hand."

His father was standing now, ready to carry out his threat, his complexion reddened with anger.

"Yes," said Thomas, his head down so that his father couldn't discern his true opinion on the matter.

"Follow me."

His father led the way out of the house, across the lawn and down the track toward the slave quarters. Striding fast and purposefully, he made no concession for his son, who struggled to keep up. Now Thomas had grown, the difference between his good leg and his bad one was even more pronounced. In the hot midday sun, beads of sweat ran down his forehead from his efforts not to lag too far behind.

As they got closer, a boy came running up behind them, overtook Thomas, and ran up to his father.

"What are you doing?"

His father turned and smiled at him. The boy was the apple of his eye, every bit his father's son in both looks and personality, a little replica George Elwood in the making.

"Come along and find out."

Thomas' half brother, Jefferson, was eleven. Thomas envied him. He could run and was athletic. Everything that Thomas wasn't and was never going to be. Jefferson would grow up to be the man his father had wanted Thomas to be.

There were several small one-room wooden shacks situated around a dusty central area. Thomas had spent many happy hours here. It was his refuge when he felt alone and unwanted in the big house, which was often.

People here always had time for him. Though Thomas realized they didn't have much choice, he believed their welcome was genuine. When he planned a visit, he would ask cook for extra food and bring it to share.

Today, the place echoed foreboding. The slaves had been brought in from the fields and stood in a silent circle.

A young man, about his own age, stood tied to the tree in the center. His back was bare. The overseer stood there, whip in hand, the strands of leather dangling like vipers eager to bite. Hearing their approach, the young man turned his head in an effort to see them. Thomas swallowed hard. It was Joshua, Maisie's eldest son. They had played together when younger. They had been friends, and were still friends in Thomas' eyes.

He saw Maisie in the crowd, her hands clasped together and resting on her chin with unspoken anxiety.

His father addressed them.

"Joshua here ran away. As you know, I am a fair master, but I will not tolerate disobedience, least of all running away. You belong to me. You are my property. I feed and house you. In return, I require loyalty, total loyalty. This time, I'll be merciful. But if Joshua runs again, if any of you run a second time, I'll chop off a foot. And you know that I never say something that I don't mean.

"Wesley, give me that. Right, Thomas, show them who's boss. Show them you're a man." George Elwood held out the whip. "Don't just stand there, boy. Take it."

Thomas reluctantly accepted it as if he was handling dynamite which could explode at any moment.

"Give him thirty of the best. Make sure you take a good long swing backward."

All eyes were upon him now. Thomas wished that he could become invisible and leave. Joshua stood facing the tree, breathing heavily in anticipation of the awful violence about to be unleashed upon him. His back glistened with droplets of perspiration, his fine skin unblemished, soon to be marked horribly for life.

Thomas took the whip back a little and swung it without force. It landed harmlessly with barely a sound on Joshua's torso.

"Harder, boy. Harder," insisted his father.

Thomas swung again but still without the power demanded of him.

"Let me try," said Jefferson eagerly.

"You may as well," sighed Elwood.

Angrily, he ripped the whip out of Thomas' hands and passed it to Jefferson, who attacked his task with glee, his eyes wild and rapacious. Despite his young age, Jefferson lashed his victim with sufficient strength to produce howls of pain. Soon Joshua's back was cut and bleeding.

"That's how you do it," said George to Thomas as if it was an act to be proud of. "That's how you earn their respect. OK, Jefferson, I'll take it from here."

Thomas gagged, swallowing the vomit which rose in his throat. He wanted to depart but knew he wouldn't be allowed. Not until Joshua was untied from the tree and had collapsed into the dirt did his father turn to go, allowing Thomas to follow along behind him and Jefferson.

Glancing back, he saw Maisie run over to her son. She noticed him looking. There was no warmth in her gaze any longer. He understood. He was part of the white folk who had done this to her son.

"Good job." George put his arm around Jefferson's shoulder. "You became a man today."

Thomas too wanted to be recognized as a man but not by hurting people. When they reached the house, Jefferson bounded up the steps to his smiling mother.

"Daddy let me whip a nigger!"

Thomas turned and limped off to the stables. Inside he found Shadow, his horse. She had a rich brown coat and big beautiful eyes with the longest eyelashes. He didn't understand why people were damned for being brown or black, while horses were treasured whatever their color. Patting her fondly, Thomas fed her some grass before saddling her.

Shadow was his legs. With her he could run, run faster than anyone. He galloped away, tears streaming down his face.

CHAPTER 8

"You're not cut out for this life, Thomas," said his father as the family sat eating dinner that evening. "I've a banking contact in Charleston. I have written to him to request that he takes you on. Sitting in an office and pouring over ledgers will be more suitable for a youth of your delicate temperament. Jefferson here is better equipped to deal with the rigors of running the plantation."

Although Thomas didn't have any desire to take over the plantation when his father died, he bristled at his plan.

"The plantation's my birthright."

"It's no such thing. My duty is to preserve this place, and I have reached the conclusion that with you at the head, its future would be in jeopardy. We'll talk no more of it."

Thomas wanted to protest, say his mother would have wanted him to inherit but he didn't. Mention of his mother was taboo. George never referred to her. When Thomas was younger and had asked his father about her, the response had been unequivocal.

"She's dead. You need to forget her. Anyway, you

have a mother, a lovely mother. My wife, Emma."

Jefferson grinned at Thomas in a supercilious way from across the table, goading him to react. Thomas wanted to go over and punch him. He resented him. Like a wolf cub that had better genes, Jefferson was the future alpha male who would force him to leave the pack.

Thomas had never been to Charleston before. Founded in 1670 and named after King Charles II of England, it was by the 1850s one of the largest American cities, and a prosperous place for those hundred or so families who held most of its wealth. Their money had in large part been derived from the slave trade. Nearly half of all the Africans kidnapped and brought to North America had come through here.

Sitting at the confluence of the Ashley and Cooper rivers, its palm trees gave it an exotic air, a place apart from the world which Thomas knew. From the vantage point of horseback, he smiled. There were fine streets of attractive mansions and church spires on the skyline. Maybe it wouldn't be so bad after all. A new place, a new start, somewhere he might find acceptance.

The city hummed with activity. Away from the main streets, that were cobbled with ballast which had been used by ships coming from England, white folk paraded on the wooden sidewalks. The black population had to keep to the muddy thoroughfare, full of puddles after one of the daily summer downpours. In the hot, damp air was the lemony fragrance of magnolia.

Thomas was to stay with Mr. Wood, a bank manager, and his family. That news had been a relief. Thomas had feared that he would be required to reside with his grandmother, the prospect of which had filled him with dread.

Having asked for directions, he found the house, which was situated behind trees not far from the center. It was a charming building with wrought iron balconies, built to catch the wind coming off the harbor and give some respite from the oppressive summer heat. A slave girl let him in. It was lunchtime and Mr. Wood was at home to eat.

"Delighted to make your acquaintance," said the tall, thin man with round eyeglasses perched on the end of his nose. He was extremely pale, no doubt a reflection of a life spent in an office. "This here's my wife, Henrietta, and these are our children, Sarah and Daniel."

"Pleased to make your acquaintance," said Thomas.

They smiled at him. It seemed a much happier family gathering than he was used to.

"Ruth, fetch another plate of food for our guest," said Henrietta to the slave girl.

"When you're done eating, she'll show you to your room and you can get some rest or wander your new neighborhood. Your father tells me that you are very studious," said the bank manager.

"I'm not sure about that, sir. Though I do enjoy reading."

"Well, there's a lot of that in banking, and writing too. How's your math?"

"Adequate I'd say."

"Good. I'll introduce you to the bank tomorrow. Banking's a sound career for a gentleman such as yourself. Did you bring a weapon with you?"

"I do have a gun."

"Good, the law requires you to carry one. There are more negroes in this town than us so we have to be ready to protect ourselves and our families. We've had the occasional uprising in our history and we don't want any more. They would slaughter us all if they had half a chance."

Thomas spent the afternoon riding around town and sitting down by the docks looking out toward the ocean, something which he had never seen before. He knew England, where most of his family's cotton went, was out there on the other side of the Atlantic, three thousand miles away. He tried to envisage how far that was but couldn't.

The following morning, Mr. Wood took him to the bank. Outside, it was an imposing building with tall columns like a Roman temple. And it was a temple of sorts, one to the god of money. Inside, clerks at desks served customers or worked on paperwork like honey bees in a hive. It felt too frenetic and suffocating for Thomas. He was used to space and nature. His heart sank at the prospect of working here.

As the newest and youngest employee he was the errand boy, which had the advantage that it got him out of the gloomy confines of the bank on a regular basis. On one occasion he was asked to go down to Ryan's Mart on Chalmers Street to collect some cash from one of the bank's most important customers, Thomas Ryan. The early morning sun had disappeared and dark thunder clouds had rolled in but Thomas didn't mind. A rain shower would bring some relief to the stifling heat until the storm ended and the humidity soared even higher.

The Mart was enclosed by high walls. He tethered Shadow and went inside. The air smelled stale, and the venue was crowded with men who had their backs to him. Thomas pushed his way through asking for Mr. Ryan.

"Up there", someone told him. Reaching the front, Thomas halted. Naively, he had imagined the Mart to be a food or livestock market. Instead, its purpose was sinister.

On a raised stage, a sorry sight greeted him. Men, women, and even children, stood shackled at the feet and neck. It was a slave market. Thomas had never visited one before. If his father sold a slave or acquired one, it was generally by word of mouth, and if he frequented such markets, he had never mentioned the fact.

Ryan was with the slaves, oblivious to the fear in their eyes. He was looking pleased with himself. There was a big crowd today which would ensure lots of sales and a handsome profit.

"What am I bid for this fine woman?" The man

grabbed her arm and pulled her forward. "Strong boned, only twenty years old. Fertile. You'll get years of work and lots of children out of her. Some of your own if you should take a liking to her."

A laugh went through the assembled men. Then the bidding started.

"Sold to the gentleman over there," said Ryan pointing to a man with a large mustache.

"Mas'r, my children, please buy them too," pleaded the woman.

"I have no need to," said her new owner. "Anyway, my overseer will be mighty pleased to give you some more for free."

Another chuckle broke out amongst the crowd.

Now unlocked from her chains, the woman bent down to hug her two young children who held her tightly as if their lives depended on it, as well they might have.

"Take her away to await her new master," Ryan commanded an assistant. Thomas overheard her parting words

"Be good my babies. Never forget your Mama loves you. I'll be thinking of you every day."

"Mama! Mama!" they cried.

As she passed by Thomas, he saw that she was silently weeping. She clearly hadn't wanted to traumatize her little ones further with her own grief. Her bravery humbled him and profoundly moved him.

He left. He had seen enough of the awful spectacle. Like the whipping of Joshua, it had been another reminder of a world which Thomas didn't want to acknowledge existed, that he didn't want to have to feel any responsibility for.

"What do you mean you didn't stay to take the money? I don't care if you felt unwell. You should've gone outside for a moment then gone back in when recovered." Elijah Wood, normally a mild tempered man was shouting. "He is one of my best customers. You will go back there immediately and apologize."

"I saw you depart," said Ryan when Thomas returned. "Is my business not to your liking?"

"No, sir," lied Thomas.

"I don't expect my bank or its employees to judge me. Do you understand, boy?"

His eyes had narrowed in a menacing way.

"Yes, sir."

"Well, don't let it happen again or I'll be speaking to Elijah about moving my account."

The years passed and Thomas became a clerk at the bank. He moved out of the Wood's house and rented a room. He wasn't the sort of person who made friends easily. However, solitude didn't bother him. Thomas preferred the company of books.

On days when he didn't have to work, he would often spend time down at the port watching ships come and go. For him, they had a magnetic allure. Vessels which could take him across the ocean. Thomas made plans to travel to Europe. He knew that it would take some years to save enough, but he was a patient character. His deformed leg had taught him to be such. One day he promised himself, one day he would get away from South Carolina and all that she represented.

CHAPTER 9

Every Christmas Thomas went home. It was the best time of year. The slaves were given a few days off and a set of new though basic clothing for the coming year. For that brief period, happiness permeated every corner of the plantation like a warm blanket keeping out the cold nights. Laughter and singing could be heard coming from the slave quarters, a contrast to the more restrained and formal atmosphere which reigned in the house. It made Thomas wonder why those with all the money seemed to have so much less capacity for joy than those who had so little.

One Christmas morning several years after he had first started working in Charleston, Thomas rose early and took Shadow out for a ride. Her breath was visible in the early morning air, coming out of her nostrils like dragon's breath. Underfoot there was a pleasing crunch from a rare frost. Low in the sky, rays of sunlight poked through the trees.

It felt good to have space after the confined streets of Charleston. Thomas galloped down toward the river and along its bank. He felt alive once more.

A tawny colored bobcat dashed across their path,

pausing briefly to hiss. Shadow balked and went up on her hind legs in fright. Thomas struggled to keep control and stay astride her. He failed and was flung into the river.

Thomas went under the cold water. Splashing around furiously, he surfaced before sinking under again. Terror gripped him. He couldn't swim and the water was fast moving from recent rains. Was this it, his life ending so quickly and unexpectedly?

He began spluttering as he took in water. He kicked with his good leg, fighting to keep his head above the surface. Try as he might he kept going back under, each time for longer than before. There was nothing he could do. He was going to drown. It seemed unreal but it wasn't.

"Over here. Grab this," a voice called.

Ahead of him, Thomas saw a large stick being held out over the water. He flailed about as he approached, fearful of missing it and being swept away to oblivion. He managed to grasp it.

The river still wanted to take him and in an instant his legs were downstream, his hands desperately clinging to his one chance of survival as he fought the force of the water. It was a battle he must win and win quickly. Thomas knew that he couldn't hold on much longer. The cold was getting to him and his strength was waning.

Whoever had the stick had begun pulling it in. He felt mud under his feet and was able to claw his way up the bank where he lay face down for a while recovering.

"Are you all right?"

He looked up to see a young woman.

"I will be," he shivered.

Shadow had arrived on the scene and stood chewing grass as though nothing had happened. Thomas got to his feet.

"You saved my life. How can I ever repay you?"

She said nothing, looking down at the ground.

"I don't recognize you. Are you new here? Look at me, please."

"I'm Mas'r Gregory's."

"What are you doing out here?"

"I like to go walking in the early morning when all is quite and a new day is dawning. I pretend things ain't what they are. That I'll soon be going back to a warm bath and a hot breakfast."

She had closed her eyes as she spoke, dreaming of her imagined world. She opened them again. The spell shattered, she looked afraid.

"Please don't tell my Mas'r. He'll be mad at me."

"Of course not. Come, get on the back of my horse. You shall have your wish."

She took a step backward.

"It's OK, you have nothing to fear. She's very friendly."

Thomas who had already climbed up onto Shadow, leaned down and grabbed his saviour under the arms and pulled her up, placing her behind him.

"Hold onto me tight."

He cantered home. After putting Shadow back in the stables, he led the young woman toward the house and into the kitchen.

"Chloe, please - what's your name?"

"Mosa."

"Please draw a warm bath for Mosa. And then give her the best and biggest breakfast you ever made. I'll be back later."

Normally garrulous, Chloe stood open mouthed in surprise, the flesh under her chin wobbling slightly. A life spent cooking had made her fat. She had to taste all that she cooked and was the only slave free to eat whatever she wanted.

Mosa had never experienced a warm bath before. She looked on in wonder as Chloe carried large pans of hot water from the stove to a metal bath in a small room nearby, creating clouds of steam as they were poured in.

"Get your clothes off and get in girl," commanded Chloe. "Here's some soap. I'll be back soon."

Mosa tentatively dipped a toe in, then climbed in and lay down. It felt like heaven as it enveloped her, so warm and comforting. This must be what it feels like to be white, she thought.

Those few minutes of bliss passed in an instant for her. Chloe reappeared.

"Ain't you washed yourself yet? Be quick. Here's a towel."

Mosa couldn't believe how soft it was and how fresh it smelled as she wrapped it around herself. She held it tightly and squeezed her eyes shut in an effort to remember this moment for always.

Back in the kitchen, she sat down to the biggest meal that she had ever eaten in her life: eggs, bacon, grits, pancakes, and butter. Chloe watched in silence as Mosa eagerly ate until Chloe's curiosity could be suppressed no longer.

"So why's Mas'r Thomas treating you like a princess? You been misbehaving with him?"

"No, not at all. His horse bucked and threw him in the river. I saw it happen and held out a stick for him to grab."

"Is that right."

Thomas returned dressed in fresh clothes.

"Don't get up," he said to Mosa as she made to stand. "Enjoy the rest of your breakfast. When you're done, I'll ride you over to the Gregory plantation."

Pouring himself some coffee from the pot by the stove, he stood watching her. Her father must have been white. Her skin was much lighter than most of the slaves.

"Do you work in the house?"

"Wish I did. I gotta work out in the fields. It's hard."

Gregory Brown's wife had probably forbidden it, thought Thomas. Not all wives would allow their husband's illegitimate children into their home.

"I oughtta leave now," said Mosa. "Thank you for my treat."

"No, thank you, Mosa. Let's get you back."

"Who's that nigger girl I saw on the back of your horse this morning?" asked Jefferson at the family breakfast.

The conversation was less restrained than usual as Emma had remained in bed with a headache.

"A man's gotta do what a man's gotta do," said George Elwood. "It'll be your turn soon enough, son."

"It's not like that. She saved my life."

"She what?" said George with only mild interest in his voice.

"Shadow was startled by a bobcat and threw me in the river. I thought I was gonna drown. She held out a stick I was able to catch hold of. I owe her my life."

"Who was it? You should reward her."

Thomas noted that his father didn't intend to do so, apparently not rejoicing that his son had survived.

"She's Gregory Brown's but I'd like to buy her. You said Chloe needs help in the kitchen. She's not worked in a house before but she seems smart."

"I suppose that could be arranged. Have you got the money?"

"I've some savings but not enough."

His plans to travel would have to wait a little longer. He was in Mosa's debt.

"I could loan you some money," said his father. "It'll need to be properly documented as a business arrangement."

"Thank you. I would appreciate that."

"OK, I'll go over and talk to Brown tomorrow.

Having a slave of your own will help teach you about the importance of property and the value of our way of life."

Thomas would have liked to buy Mosa to free her. However, the invention of the cotton gin by Eli Whitney at the end of the eighteenth century had been a curse for freedom. The engine's ability to remove seeds from cotton, previously a laborious manual process, had made it a boom crop, greatly expanding its cultivation and making it the bedrock of the Southern economy.

That in turn had resulted in Southern states severely restricting the ability to manumit slaves, fearful that it would result in an insufficient supply of labor. Some states prohibited the freeing of a

slave except by will. South Carolina had gone even further, requiring a legislative approval to a manumission, effectively ending the practice.

"He says she's yours for eight hundred dollars on account of her saving you, but warns she can be a lazy one," reported back his father. "You can go collect her at any time."

Later that day, Thomas brought her back.

"Let me show you your room in the attic. You need to take these back stairs up and down, never the main ones or you'll get yourself into trouble," explained Thomas as he hauled himself up stair by stair, always having to lead with his good leg. "Well, here it is. Ain't much, but maybe better than what you're used to."

"Oh it sure is, and none of Eliza's kids to take care of after a day's work."

The room was barely bigger than the single bed in there, but to her it was a dream come true. Her very own room. Thomas noticed her shabby clothes.

"I'll get a new dress for you. Now let's go give Chloe the news. Don't be put off, her bark is worse than her bite."

"A field hand! What can I be doing with a field hand who can't cook."

"She's eager to learn," said Thomas.

"Well, you better be girl, and quick to learn. I ain't got time to do things over if you make a mess of them."

"You'll be a wonderful teacher, Chloe. If she learns to cook half as good as you do, she'll be in great demand."

"Oh be off with you and your flattery."

"I must go back to Charleston tomorrow. I'll be back in a few months to check how it's all going. Make sure you do as Chloe tells you, Mosa, and I know you'll do well."

Word of the new arrival soon spread.

"They got a new girl in the house working for Chloe in the kitchen," Nathaniel informed Maisie a couple of days later as they ate cornbread for dinner off of the rough wooden table that he had made. "Mosa's her name."

The news was like a punch to her abdomen. The shock was intense. Rarely had she thought of the girl since handing her to Ella all those years ago. Putting the past out of her mind had made her feel safe. She had no reason to believe Mosa would ever return.

"You're awful quiet woman. Ain't like you to have nothing to say."

"I'm just feeling a little off. I'm gonna get me some fresh air."

Maisie wandered toward the house. The drapes were closed. She stood there, pulling at her hair with worry. In there were father and daughter. The daughter who he believed had died long ago. If George Elwood ever discovered the new help in the kitchen was his, Maisie's world would come crashing down like a stick house in a hurricane.

CHAPTER 10

Thomas thought of Mosa as he rode through the darkness back to Charleston. What was it about her that made him feel so protective toward her, that made his heart skip a beat? Perhaps it was the mesmerizing effect of those large eyes whenever she lifted her head and looked up at him, her eyelids slowly retracting in an almost sultry way.

Whatever it was, he couldn't seem to get her out of his mind. There was a certain grace and elegance about the way she carried herself which enchanted him.

Since arriving in Charleston, he hadn't gone home often. It was a good day's ride, two if he wanted to do it in comfort. Now he began returning every month.

"You seem to be coming home more frequently than I change my undergarments," said his father in an unusually jovial mood. "You seeing some gal round here? It's time you thought about marriage and settling down."

"One day, when I meet the right girl. I like coming back to escape Charleston. It's awful humid down on the coast."

Chloe had her suspicions too.

"Mas'r Thomas seems mighty keen on you," she commented as she vigorously chopped at a large hunk of meat with a cleaver.

"I don't know what you mean," said Mosa, who was washing dishes and standing with her back to Chloe, enabling her to hide the weakness of her denial.

"I think you do."

And she did. She appreciated his kindness. Few people had ever shown her much consideration. Thomas was different. Maybe his disability made him more sensitive to the needs of others, or perhaps it made him identify with those who were regarded as inferior.

The times when he came home, he would tell Chloe that he needed Mosa's help and take her off on his horse. They would find a quiet spot to tether Shadow and talk as they walked.

"I wish I could free you, Mosa, but the law won't allow it. It now requires a special decree from the State Legislature."

"Well, I doubt that's gonna be happening any time soon."

"I could take you North. It wouldn't be like escaping. There'd be nothing to fear. No one would stop us, a master and his slave. What do you say?"

"I don't know. What could I do up there? I can't even read or write."

"I can teach you."

"Wouldn't you get into trouble? It's against the

law."

"No one need ever know."

"OK. Then maybe once I can read and write, I could go."

That night Mosa lay in bed unable to sleep, thinking of a new life, a life of freedom. Every slave dreamed of that, getting North to a supposed land of milk and honey where no one owned you. But the prospect frightened her too. Her entire life had been spent on a plantation, her horizons small and contained. The outside world seemed too big a place, too easy to get lost in. And she had been conditioned to think that she was worth nothing, incapable of achieving anything.

Over the next year and a half, whenever Thomas was home and Mosa had finished her chores for the day, they would sneak over to the stables and sit amongst the hay. To a background of horses chomping and farting, he taught her how to read and write by candlelight.

In the cozy shadows, he would watch Mosa. Her eyes down, intently focused on reading. Thomas was able to observe her without her noticing, savor the moment and replay it time and again as he thought about her when he retired to bed.

He would delight in her hearty laugh when she mispronounced a word and he had told her the correct pronunciation. She made him feel happy, something he hadn't felt for so long.

As she grew in confidence, he let her keep whichever book he had brought from the house.

"Be careful to hide it and return it to the library when you're finished with it. Do it when everyone's sleeping."

Mosa's heart would thump with trepidation each time she sneaked into the room late at night to return a book. She would run her fingers along the book spines, breathing in the musty aroma. To her, it was the sweetest smell of all.

Learning to read had opened her mind to the possibilities which life could have. Gaining knowledge for Mosa was like collecting precious artefacts or accumulating money. It was her key to a new and better life.

"Where's Mosa?" said Emma storming into the kitchen one morning.

"She's out back peeling vegetables ma'am," answered Chloe. "I'll go get her for you."

Mosa wondered what she could have done to annoy Mrs. Elwood when she saw her standing there, her lips narrow and arms folded.

"Mosa, have you been at our books?"

Mosa felt herself become clammy in an instant. The mistress of the house would be furious if she had discovered what Mosa was up to.

"I...I move them when I'm dusting."

"Well, make sure they go back in their proper places. You left a red one in amongst the blue ones. You may not be able to read but I take it you're not colorblind?"

"No, ma'am."

"Then don't let it happen again."

Chloe raised her eyebrows after Emma Elwood had departed, but the prompt for a confession failed.

"Be careful, chile. You got a good job here in the house. Don't go ruining it."

On one visit, Thomas appeared excited with the choice of reading material which he had brought.

"This novel is taking the country by storm; well, the North at least. They say it's sold more copies than any book other than the Bible. It's called *Uncle Tom's Cabin*. It's about the evils of slavery by a lady called Harriet Beecher Stowe. It's hard to find a copy in the South but I managed to. Look after it for me until next time."

In her tiny room, Mosa wept as she read of the heartaches of the slave characters depicted in the book. To her it was no novel. It was reality, her reality, the reality of millions like her. She wanted to leave now. She was ready.

"It's incredible how well you've done these past months. You're right it's time for you to go," said Thomas on his next visit as they sat amongst the horses once again. "I'm sure gonna miss you though, but I'll be happy knowing that you'll be free and able to achieve all that you're capable of."

"Thank you, Thomas, for doing this. I'll miss you too."

"I'll be back as soon as I can, and then we'll ride North. I'll stay with you until we find you work and a place to live. Hey, I almost forgot. I brought you a gift."

"A gift?"

Mosa had never been given a present before. It was small, wrapped in brown paper and tied with a red ribbon.

"A book," she said beaming as she opened it.

"Yes, a book of poetry. I have the same one and like it very much. I thought if we each read it before bedtime, we can do so in the knowledge that the other one is doing the same, even after you're long gone and hundreds of miles away up North."

Mosa's face crumpled as if she were about to cry.

"We ought to get back to the house," said Thomas. It was a warm summer night. Though the moon was but a thin sliver, thousands of stars gave light enough to see the silhouettes of trees and fences.

"Look up, Mosa. There's the Milky Way I was telling you about. Isn't it incredible?"

"Just wonderful."

A cosmic cloud of light was spread across the heavens. A reminder of the wonder of the universe, of the opportunities life could offer when you weren't held back by someone else's tyranny.

They looked at each other. Each felt a desire, a hunger. Their lips met in a soft, uncertain kiss. A kiss that ignited a wish for more.

A cough startled them. Somebody must be nearby. Embarrassed, they broke apart.

"I must be getting back. Chloe left me some cleaning up to do."

Mosa ran off into the darkness. Thomas stayed a while looking up at the sky, a surge of excitement and nerves coursing through his veins.

Two crept away, neither having seen the other. One went, her head weighed down with worry. She had to stop this. They were brother and sister. The problem was how to. If the truth came out the consequences would be devastating for her.

The other took a circuitous route back to the house, enjoying the warm feeling in his groin. Seeing them kissing had aroused him. His brother would soon be back in Charleston.

CHAPTER 11

Dragonflies hovered over the water dancing like tiny ballerinas as Mosa strolled by the river. In her hand she held the little book of poems which Thomas had given her.

Life was good. Like a flower in spring, her world was about to open. Her long winter of captivity and emptiness would soon be over. She didn't know when Thomas would return but she knew he would. He was a man of his word.

She imagined her new life of freedom, what it would be like to be free, to go wherever she wanted, to buy clothes and look pretty. Mosa had already decided that when she had accrued some spare money, her first purchase would be a mirror. She had never got to look at herself properly. Only the occasional furtive glance when she passed the mirror in the hall, afraid that if she stood to look at herself one of the Elwoods would catch her and berate her.

Her daydreaming was halted abruptly.

"Give me that. That's not yours. You ain't allowed books. How many other things have you been stealing from us?"

Jefferson snatched the book from her and threw it in the water. The look in his eyes scared her. It was more than a reprimand for reading. His gaze was unrestrained, feral like a rutting stag. He seized her arm.

"Come on. Give me a kiss. Like you do him."

She pulled away.

"Hey! You don't refuse me. We own you."

He dragged her into the trees, ignoring her pleas of 'please stop' and her sobbing as he forced himself on her.

Mosa lay there in trauma after he had gone. She felt dead inside. In an instant, all the joy in her world had been extinguished.

She was shaking as she returned to the house. Taking a deep breath and pushing her shoulders back, she wiped the tears from her face as she steeled herself to enter the kitchen.

"Is you all right?" asked Chloe. "You look sick."

"It'll pass."

Slaves had to be virtually on their death bed to be excused from a day's work. Mosa kept her back to Chloe as she did her chores. Chloe couldn't read a book, but she could read people's faces.

"Cat got your tongue? You're awful quiet this morning."

"Just tired I guess."

"He ain't got you pregnant, has he?"

"Who?"

Internally, Mosa took another blow. What if his brother had? A part of him that would grow inside her. Someone to remind her forever of what had happened this morning.

"Mas'r Thomas of course, less you been fooling around with somebody else too."

"I ain't been fooling around with nobody, Mas'r Thomas included. I just don't feel that good. I'm not in the mood for talking."

"Hmm," said Chloe.

I have to go right now. I can't wait for Thomas to come back. If I stay, his brother will come after me again, thought Mosa as she kneaded dough to make bread. She hoped Chloe would remain on the other side of the kitchen and not notice the tears falling onto the worktop.

That evening after Chloe had retired, Mosa stayed in the kitchen and placed a few pieces of food in a cloth which she tied into a small bag. She had only a vague idea of which way was North, and no real sense of how far she would need to travel to reach freedom but she had to try.

Quietly, she went off into the night. Soon the river blocked her way. Better to drown here than be raped again. Tentatively, she waded in. The water crept ever higher up her legs and made her dress billow, liquid chains that wouldn't ever let her go. She waited for the river to overpower her, sweep her downstream and pull her down, down. However, even midstream it came no higher than her waist. Mosa exhaled, releasing her fear. She was going to make it.

When morning came, she ate some of the food

which she had brought. Having crossed another river a little earlier, she felt safe enough to take a nap in the forest. She only meant to sleep a few minutes.

The barking of dogs woke her. She got up and began to run but they had her scent. As she crashed through the trees, branches scratched her face and arms. Mosa didn't notice. The adrenaline of terror drove her on.

The yelping was becoming louder. Looking behind, she saw them closing on her. Ahead was a tree with a spindly trunk she could get her arms around. Mosa hauled herself up it, hanging on for dear life as the dogs, teeth bared, snarled and growled at her, their jumps reaching to less than a foot beneath her.

Not long afterward, the overseer and a couple of his men arrived on their horses. He called off the dogs and Mosa came down. With her hands tied to a piece of rope, she had to run to keep from falling and being dragged along the ground as they trotted back to the plantation.

Retribution was swift. She screamed in agony as the leather tore at the flesh on her bare back. Mosa wondered what she had done to deserve a life like this. No parents to love her, no one to keep her safe, unprotected from rape and violence.

Condemned to be used and abused, she was in hell. Mosa wished she had never saved Thomas that day, wished that she had remained unnoticed working in the fields on Gregory Brown's plantation.

The pain dulled over time, though her back would never be soft and silky like it once was. It was her mind which didn't heal. Dawn no longer brought the promise of a new day to be discovered. Instead, it brought her only a dread in the pit of her stomach, dread that Jefferson would come looking for her again.

Mosa resolved to use her fear to make herself strong, resolved not to let herself be a victim ever again. Her difference had taught her of the need to rely on herself, not others. She wasn't part of a family. No one had her back. She couldn't call on law enforcement or seek justice. There was no such thing for her. There was only one thing that she could do.

Late one evening, Mosa slipped out of her bed in the attic and went down to the kitchen. The cat kept to catch rats which came in search of food let out a loud miaow as she stepped on its tail in the dark. She froze. Chloe's room was right next to the kitchen. However, her snoring continued unabated.

Carefully, Mosa opened the door to her room. There on the wall next to the door hung keys. Gently, she lifted them off the hook and went back into the kitchen. Feeling with her hands, she found the drawer and the keyhole.

Mosa pulled out the biggest, sharpest one. She would clean it off and return it when she was done. No one need know that it had been used.

Mosa opened the kitchen door to depart. This time it creaked. She decided to leave it open. Closing it again at this juncture was too risky.

Stealthily, she climbed the staircase to their floor. The floor beneath hers where they slept with feather pillows and the softest of cotton sheets, not the torn and threadbare bedding and straw pillow which she had.

Mosa knew which door. She turned the doorknob and entered. Light from the moon came through the partially closed drapes. He lay on his back, mouth open, unsuspecting. His sheets were pulled back to his waist, his nightshirt open and revealing enough of his chest.

She raised the knife with two hands above her head, ready to plunge with all the force that she could muster.

CHAPTER 12

Mosa wavered, psyching herself up to complete the task. As she did so, someone grabbed her from behind.

"Stop. Give it to me."

She recognized the voice and complied. Thomas led her quietly out of the room and downstairs, telling her to wait outside the back door while he put back the knife.

"What on earth did you think you were doing?" he asked stepping out into the night. "You would hang for that."

"He…he attacked me. He raped me."

She began crying. Thomas moved forward and held her in his arms.

"I'm here now. You're safe." He waited for her to become calmer. "Go to bed and get some rest. I'll deal with him in the morning."

Thomas knew Jefferson was a habitual late riser these days. When Thomas heard his father and Emma go downstairs, he made his move.

"Wake up," he said, shaking his half-brother.

"What do you think you're doing?" Jefferson sat up in his bed, a scowl on his face.

"You're going to pay for your crime."

"Crime? Have you lost your mind?"

"You violated Mosa."

"Your nigger whore. And what if I did? She enjoyed it, told me I was much better than you."

"A duel. I challenge you to a duel."

Thomas was almost snorting with rage, the vein in his forehead pulsing, his cheeks flushed.

"A duel with my crippled brother? I accept the challenge. And when you lay dying, remember who'll be laying with her tonight. I'll see you down by Joseph's Creek at eleven. I'll bring Jones to officiate."

"I'll be there."

"Good. I'll bring pistols from father's study. This is for real you know. A chance to settle things between us once and for all."

Thomas was there ten minutes early. Joseph's Creek was out of sight of the house, hidden amongst trees which kept the place in shadow. Along the side of the creek was grass. The two brothers would walk along it, starting back to back. For one of them, it would be his very last walk.

It seemed as though the flies could smell Thomas' tension. They buzzed around him, ignoring his repeated efforts to swipe them away.

A smirk on his face, Jefferson turned up with Jones, the overseer, five minutes late. Jones opened both of the pistols to demonstrate that each was loaded with six bullets.

"You can choose," said Jefferson.

Thomas picked one, hoping his brother wouldn't notice his shaking hand as he took it, but he did and tried to unsettle him more.

"I saw Jeremiah as I left the house. I told him to get a coffin and some helpers down here later. I'm not carrying your body back. It's too far."

"Gentlemen," said Jones, "Do you wish to reconsider?"

"No," they both answered without hesitation.

"Then stand back to back and walk twenty paces. When I tell you to turn, you may do so and begin firing."

Jones counted the paces. Thomas fought to control his nerves. He had never had his brother's self-confidence. Droplets of cold sweat ran in lines down his torso.

He had to be strong. If he failed, Mosa would be defenseless. He should have just let her kill his brother. He could have said that he did it if she were accused. But it was too late now for second thoughts.

"...eighteen, nineteen, twenty."

There was silence. It was as though time itself had come to a halt.

"You may turn and fire," shouted the overseer.

Jefferson made the first shot. It got Thomas in the upper left arm. He fought his urge to flinch; he mustn't lose his concentration. He ignored the pain. Focused, he aimed and fired.

His aim was true. Jefferson fell to the ground

clutching his chest.

"No!" George Elwood had come running with Jeremiah. George fell on his knees beside the young man. "Jefferson, Jefferson. Wake up."

But his face was a ghostly white and his eyes were closed. His head flopped to one side as George Elwood raised his son's shoulders to embrace him.

Thomas hadn't moved as if glued to the spot.

"What have you done?"

"It was an honorable duel."

"A duel? What in God's name for?"

"He raped Mosa."

"You believed her, over your brother? That girl has brought a curse upon this family."

"I'm taking her and leaving. I love her. We're going North. I'm going to find a place where I can marry her."

"You will do no such thing."

"She's mine. I can do what I like."

"No, you cannot. She remains registered in my name. She's my property."

"But you agreed when I paid back the loan, she'd be mine. We signed an agreement."

"Prove it. You don't have a copy. Jeremiah, fetch help. We need to get Jefferson home."

CHAPTER 13

Thomas left, hobbling toward the house. He had just killed his half brother, but Thomas felt no regret, no guilt, and strangely calm. As he walked, he formed a plan. He would ride to the doctor's in town and get his arm fixed. Then tonight, he and Mosa would ride North and keep going until they were out of the slave States.

Emma stood on the front steps wringing her hands as she watched Jeremiah call for a couple of others to help him.

"What's happened? Where's Jefferson?"

"Down by Joseph's Creek," said Thomas holding the rail to climb the steps.

Emma rushed past him, raising her skirt off the ground as she ran. Thomas went inside and flung open the kitchen door, startling Mosa and Chloe.

"Come outside."

Mosa followed.

"It's done. He won't ever bother you again."

Mosa placed her hand over her mouth.

"It's OK. I challenged him to a duel. He accepted. Legally they can't touch me."

"You're hurt," said Mosa noticing the blood on his

arm.

"It's not too bad. Listen, I'll ride into Columbia to see the doctor. When I return, we'll leave and go North. I can't live in this place any longer. We can be together. If you want, I mean."

Mosa nodded.

News of the fraternal killing and the reason for it spread through the plantation like wildfire. It passed along the cotton fields faster than someone could run.

"He said he loved her. Was leaving with her and going North to marry her."

"Marry her?" repeated Maisie as if saying it again would make it untrue.

"Yes, marry her," said the woman working next to Maisie.

Maisie put her head back down and carried on picking, but her hands were trembling.

That evening as the light was fading, Thomas returned. He didn't know why but he felt a sense of foreboding as he saw someone standing there, a figure outlined against the sinking sun. Who was it? It wasn't Mosa. What could have happened?

"Maisie?" he asked as her features became visible.

"Mas'r Thomas, we need to talk."

He slid down from his horse.

"I was there the night your sister was born."

"What of it? She died."

"No, she didn't. It was Mosa."

"Maisie, has too much sun made you insane?"

"It's true. Your mother gave birth to a brown baby

girl. Your daddy was mad. Madder than I ever seen him. He told me to take the girl and drown her in the river, and never speak of it. Never, or he'd sell me away from my family. I couldn't kill the child, so I took her to the Brown plantation and left her there. They asked me what to call her. I said Mosa. Talk is you dun said you gonna marry Mosa. But you can't. She's your sister."

"That's not possible."

"You'd think so. But I heard the doctor talking to your daddy. He said it's possible that if there's mixed race somewhere in your ancestry, it can unexpectedly show up many years later. How else could your Mama deliver a brown baby? And even if your daddy weren't the father, she's still your half-sister."

Thomas' shoulders sank. The energy and vitality which had exhilarated him on the ride back as he thought of a future together with Mosa evaporated into thin air like drops of water on the leaves after a summer storm. He said nothing as his mind tried to process the enormity of what he had just heard.

He thought of Mosa's features. Her thin nose and the bump in the middle. He had never paid any attention to the comparison, but it was just like his father's. And the shape of her mouth. It was identical even if her smile was so much brighter. And those doleful eyes, weren't they the same as Thomas' very own.

"But what about the funeral? I was there. They

buried my sister, next to my mother."

"All I know is your sister lived. She weren't in that box they put in the ground."

"And my mother?"

"She died in hospital. Your daddy took her there the night of the birth."

"We need to open her coffin."

"Lord no. You can't go digging up the dead. They'll haunt you forever."

"I'll do it alone then."

"Promise me you'll never say anything that'll make your father send me away. Being sold and separated from my family would be worse than dying."

"I swear I won't, Maisie. On my life."

Maisie left. She felt relief. That burden which had consumed her for so long was gone. But once more the relief proved to be temporary. Before she reached her shack, she was already wishing that she had kept quiet. The consequences of what she had just done were beyond her control, and that made her extremely anxious.

CHAPTER 14

Thomas remained by the stables. A gut-wrenching grief welled up inside him, but it was a grief which he would have to hide from the world. The woman who Thomas loved, had planned to marry somehow, he could love no more. Not in the way he wanted to. His love could be only a platonic one.

He led Shadow into the stables. While she drank, he beat one of the wooden supports with his fists and shouted with rage. Thomas couldn't face Mosa this evening. He couldn't face anyone.

Thomas stayed there until it was dark, and then made his way over to the family graveyard carrying a large spade. Though visible from the house, the drapes were all closed. They had been since this morning as Emma and his father mourned the loss of their son and heir.

There were three tombstones inside an enclosure surrounded by a low white picket fence; his grandfather's, his mother's, and what he had grown up believing was his sister's. Soon his brother's would make a fourth.

Thomas approached his mother's grave with apprehension. Looking around at regular intervals to check that there was still no one about, he cut into the grass and under it. Wincing with each dig from the pain of his wound where he had been shot, he removed the turf piece by piece and then dug out the earth. There was a clunk as he hit wood. Scraping the soil away, he got his spade under the lid of the coffin and levered it open. Cloth was wrapped around the contents.

Now on his knees on the edge of the hole, he leaned forward. Thomas felt nauseous. He had never seen a skeleton before. This was wrong. Maisie was right. Seeing what little would remain of his mother's corpse after so many years would be something he could never unsee. It would haunt him.

Yet the urge to know proved too much. He pulled the cloth away gradually, ready to throw it back as soon as the first bones became visible. But there were none, only planks of wood, cut to fit inside the coffin.

He sat up and put his head in his hands. His mother wasn't buried here, so just where had she been buried? Thrown into an unmarked grave like a pauper, disowned by her husband in death as in life?

Thomas closed the lid of the coffin and shoveled back in the soil which he had piled beside him before carefully replacing the turf.

Standing there, he scratched his head for inspiration. After brushing the dirt from his hands, he went into the house and entered his father's office. The man was a meticulous keeper of paper. If there was any record of what had happened to his mother's body, he would find it here.

Shutting the door, he lit a candle and in the flickering light began searching through the drawers of the desk. There were bills and papers for the slaves that his father had bought and sold, and for supplies of goods, and sales of cotton but nothing concerning his mother.

One drawer wouldn't open, it was locked. Thomas scanned the desktop for a key but couldn't see one.

He moved a pile of books on the left side of the desk to look at the papers underneath them. The last but one book stuck to the bottom one. As Thomas pulled it up, it lifted the front cover of the book beneath. It was a false book, a place to hide things. Inside was a set of keys.

One fitted the drawer. Opening it, he took out the papers it contained. A collection of invoices. From a business in Savannah, Georgia. The Baynham Asylum. Fees for an Ethel Smith.

In five minutes Thomas was gone, galloping toward Charleston. He was there by early morning and down at the railway station. Leaving Shadow to be cared for, he took the all-day train journey to Savannah.

Arriving early evening, he took a room in a hotel and hired a horse so that he could wander the city without anyone noticing his cumbersome gait. The Asylum was outside the town. He would go there in the morning.

Savannah appeared to be smaller than Charleston. It was a town of over twenty attractive squares, many with fountains and statues. The charming layout was thanks to an English general, James Oglethorpe, who had founded the city in 1733 as the first settlement in the new colony of Georgia, and who had meticulously planned its development.

However, in the overbearing humidity of summer, that charm was lost. Palmetto bugs, like flying cockroaches, and myriads of mosquitoes cut short Thomas' sightseeing, driving him back to the hotel.

Large oak trees with Spanish moss hanging from them lined the streets in abundance, like cobwebs in a house which had been shut for years. Thomas noticed a preponderance of light blue

dwellings, painted with indigo and buttermilk. It was thought that kept the ghosts away, a fellow guest at the hotel told him.

There was more than a hint of otherworldliness about Savannah; a taste of mystery, or was it malevolence?

Come bedtime, he hoped the cheesecloth at his window would keep out the insects. A night spent sweating behind closed windows seemed worse than the risk of their bites. However, even with an open window, the air had the consistency of molasses.

Tormented by his recent discoveries, he slept fitfully. His world, which had seemed to offer such promise only a couple of days ago, was in turmoil, turned upside down by revelations he never could have imagined.

The following morning, the innkeeper gave him directions to the asylum. It was discreetly positioned down a densely forested track. With loud shrieks, birds warned each other of his approach.

The building was brick and had bars on the windows. Thomas rang the bell and a young black woman opened the door.

"Good morning. I've been sent by Mr. George Elwood to check on Ethel Smith."

"Please wait here, sir."

She walked down the corridor and out of sight. An unpleasant smell of urine permeated a stagnant atmosphere. There was no sign of another human being. Occasional shouts and screams rang out from behind closed doors.

A man with an untidy thicket of red hair appeared from a side door.

"Good morning, sir. I am Elias O' Toole. And you?"

"Tobias Elwood, a nephew of Mr. George Elwood."

"I understand that you wish to see Ethel Smith on behalf of Mr. Elwood. I don't recall any such request previously being made, and I have been here five years."

"My uncle knew that I would be passing through Savannah on my way to Florida, and asked if I might call as no one has been to visit her for some considerable time."

"May I inquire if you have a letter of authority?"

His manner was obsequious.

"Indeed I do."

Thomas passed him the handwritten note which he had forged. Deliberately he gave it to the man upside down. O'Toole didn't seek to turn it around. He merely screwed up his eyes pretending to read it.

"That all seems to be in order. I will take you up. Please follow me."

There were no soothing touches. The walls were without pictures, the paint peeling and marked, the staircase and corridors unvarnished and devoid of rugs.

O'Toole jangled his keys as he went, a jailor in all but name. He stopped outside a room on the second floor.

"I should warn you that Miss Smith is quite unsettled."

"May I see her alone?"

"I suppose that will be all right. I shall wait at the bottom of the stairs. Call for me should you need me or when you are ready to leave."

He unlocked the door. Thomas waited until O'Toole had begun to descend the staircase before opening it. Like the hall outside, the room was undecorated and lacked any comfort. A narrow bed and upright wooden chair were all that it contained.

A woman in a stained and once white nightdress stood looking out of the window. Her long hair, which hung down her back uncombed and unwashed, was gray.

As Thomas shut the door behind him, she turned. Her face was emaciated and wrinkled, making her look much older than the fifty years of age she must now be. She opened her mouth as if to speak. Many of her teeth had fallen out. Those that remained were yellow.

It had been almost twenty years but he knew who she was.

"Mother."

Thomas went to embrace her. She drew back, flattening herself against the window.

"Don't be frightened. It's me, Thomas. Your son."

Jane made a plaintive whimpering sound. But it wasn't a sound of grief or joy at finally getting to see her son after all these years. There was no hint of recognition in her eyes, instead only a look of wide-eyed terror.

"Help. Help me," she yelled. "I'm being attacked."

She took hold of the chair and raised it as if she meant to break it over his head. O'Toole came running.

"She's having one of her turns. Be calm now, Ethel," he said authoritatively. "Give me the chair. No one is going to hurt you. That's it. Now lie down."

Like a dog, she went to the bed and lay down, curling up. She looked up at them both, expressionless.

Thomas turned away and went out into the corridor to hide his anguish. He put his hands on the wall for support and hung his head.

"I'm sorry," said O'Toole as he emerged and locked the door, "It's like I said, she's unsettled."

Thomas didn't look at him and walked toward the staircase.

"I've seen enough. I'll let my uncle know of her condition."

Reaching the ground floor, he quickly left the building. He rode back to Savannah, bewildered at how his life had changed so much and so quickly.

CHAPTER 15

Thomas took the train back to Charleston. For the duration of the journey, he sat with his head facing outward. He had no wish to engage in conversation with fellow passengers. His life had become a nightmare. He would have felt better if he had discovered that his mother was dead as he had always believed. To see the person who she had become was deeply distressing.

Eventually, exhaustion overcame him. Thomas fell asleep, waking only when the guard touched his arm to wake him at their destination after the other passengers had already disembarked.

It was late in the evening, but Thomas knew that he wouldn't be able to sleep so he saddled up once again and rode the familiar route back to the plantation, arriving the next morning.

His desire to confront his father immediately was thwarted as he saw mourners dressed in black standing around the latest addition to the family plot. Outside the enclosure the slaves stood, forced to pay homage to someone for whom they could surely have had not one ounce of respect.

Those who mourned didn't see him. Some of the

slaves did. Thomas saw Maisie look in his direction. He knew if she could have spoken, she would have implored him to say nothing to his father. Giving her a nod to reassure her, he slipped quietly into the house and up to his room where he lay down and fell fast asleep.

Waking up, he could hear the muffled noise of guests repeating their condolences as they departed. Through his window he watched a long line of carriages roll away kicking up the dust as they did so.

"I'm going up to my room," he heard Emma call out to his father.

As soon as she had shut her door, Thomas went downstairs searching for the man. He found him in his study, sitting at his desk.

"You have a nerve showing your face here. Especially today of all days."

"I do? How about you? I've been to Savannah to see someone. Your wife, your real wife. My mother."

His father sat back in his chair as though trying to dodge a bullet.

"How could you? Pretend to a young boy that his mother was dead."

Thomas was careful to make no mention of his sister still being alive for Maisie's sake.

"Your mother disgraced this family. She had a brown baby. Most men would have killed their wives with their bare hands for that."

"How do you know that she wasn't yours?"

"How could she be?"

"Mixed race in our ancestry."

"What's your grandmother been saying?"

"So it is true."

"It seems it might be."

"You know it's true, so why did you punish mom?"

"I didn't know until afterward, when it was too late. Everyone thought she'd been buried."

"So you just left her to rot in an asylum and remarried. Do you know how long you'll spend in prison for this?"

George felt for the drawer handle, pulled it open and wrapped his right hand around the metal. An angry son, one who'd already killed his brother, it wouldn't be hard to portray it as self-defense. But Thomas had noticed. He threw himself over the desk onto his father, knocking him off his chair onto the floor.

Thomas picked up the gun and stood. Still lying there, George put his hands up to his face, palms facing outwards in surrender.

"Don't shoot."

"Relax. I'm not going to kill you. But here's what you will do. You'll get mom moved out of that hell hole in Savannah and brought up to Charleston to a decent place where she can be cared for one on one in comfort."

"And you won't tell anyone what happened?"

"So long as you do all I ask. And don't even think of killing me as I'll leave a letter with my will to be opened on my death recounting all that you've done. You'll sign Mosa over to me. Now. We'll be leaving tonight."

"I can't."

"Can't or won't."

"I sold her."

CHAPTER 16

Mosa had tried to keep out of sight since the duel. When the family found out that she was the cause of it, there was no telling what they would do to her.

She wanted to run and hide but Thomas had told her he would be back tonight. There were just a few more hours to wait. Mosa had waited her whole life for freedom. She only had to wait such a short time now.

That evening, Mosa went to go up to her room to get her things. She stopped at the bottom of the back stairs. There was nothing to collect, only another dress which was old and frayed. She had no mementos, nothing of value, sentimental or otherwise.

That didn't make her sad, however. She had a future now. She could read and write. She could find a job. A teacher maybe, that would be a good career. Mosa could give the gift of reading and writing to others, give them a chance to get on in life.

And there was Thomas. So kind and gentle that she could forget who his family was. He was a man Mosa could trust. Though just what would happen between them she didn't know. She didn't want to be some man's mistress. Could it be they allowed mixed marriages in the North? She found that hard to believe.

Mosa remained in the kitchen waiting. She stayed there all night, becoming increasingly concerned when Thomas didn't return.

"You's up early for once," said Chloe coming into the kitchen bleary eyed.

"I couldn't sleep."

"Well, you can start making their breakfast."

When she was done, Mosa stepped outside to take in the early morning air. She was sweating from cooking and anxiety. Looking out across the fields and toward the track which he would come riding down, she breathed in deeply in an effort to calm her nerves. It wasn't long until her prayers were answered. She saw movement in the distance and her spirits soared. It must be him. Finally, she would get away from here.

"Thank you, Lord," she whispered.

But as the person and his transport assumed a clear shape, she began to have doubts. The man was driving a horse and cart. Thomas would surely be on Shadow.

Soon he was close enough for her to make out the reason for a cart. He had a cargo. Shackled and silent. It wasn't Thomas. It was a slave trader.

The arrival of such a man would cause a collective shiver to run down the spines of those working on a plantation. Owners usually only sold once a year if they had suffered a poor harvest and needed to raise money. But the passing slave trader could catch them on a whim. Persuade them to make a quick buck, get rid of someone they saw as being too much trouble.

Mosa retreated to the house. Thomas would surely be here any minute. The doctor must have told him to rest the night in town. He wouldn't be long now.

Jeremiah appeared in the kitchen.

"Mas'r George wants to see you out front."

Mosa's heart missed a beat. She looked behind her at the kitchen door. She should have gone last night when Thomas didn't come. It was too late to run.

George Elwood stood outside the front of the house with the trader, who grinned lasciviously when he saw Mosa.

"She'll do fine."

"Yes, you've got yourself a bargain at five hundred dollars."

"It's been a pleasure doing business with you, sir."

George went back into the house without even looking at Mosa. To him she was pure evil, the cause of his son's death. She had bewitched his other son, beguiled him into killing his own brother. That his favorite son should perish for forcing himself upon a slave girl was beyond the man's comprehension. It happened all the time without any consequence.

"Come Missi."

Mosa drew back. The trader marched over and hit her hard across the face. She fell to the ground. Grabbing her by the arm, he pulled her up.

"You're mine now. No more fancy airs and graces. You do as I say. End of story. I've met your sort before. Uppity niggers. Just 'cos you got a bit of white blood in you, you think you're something special. Well, you ain't, you're a nigger just like the rest of them."

He manhandled her into the back of the cart and locked shackles around her legs and neck. Her fellow passengers didn't even turn to look at her. They were each lost in their own world of despair. Mosa recognized a man from the Brown plantation.

The cart trundled off. The slave trader stopped only once that day to give them some water and let them relieve themselves. He afforded them no dignity. They were forced to go still shackled and next to each other.

With each bump in the track, Mosa was getting farther away from Thomas. And even should his father reveal who she had been sold to, how would Thomas ever find her? Sold to an itinerant slave trader, there was no trail for him to follow. She was disappearing into that oblivion slaves who were sold were cast into. Sent to a place which they couldn't ever leave and unable to communicate their whereabouts, forever lost.

CHAPTER 17

"Sold her? What do you mean sold her?" demanded Thomas.

"I sold her the day before yesterday. She's caused so much bad blood in our family," said his father.

"She? Mosa did nothing wrong. Jefferson caused the bad blood by raping her. Who'd you sell her to?"

"That's none of your business."

"It most certainly is if you want the family secret kept that way."

"It was some trader passing through."

"Where was he taking her?"

"I don't know."

"I'm not buying that for a minute. Don't lie to me. Have no doubt, I won't hesitate-"

"He said he was taking her to Ryan's Mart in Charleston."

"Give me fifteen hundred dollars. I'm gonna buy her back."

"Fifteen hundred dollars! I only sold her for five hundred."

"Too bad."

"I don't know that I have that much cash."

"Well, you better find it if you don't want Emma to know that her marriage is null and void, and that her son was a bastard."

George unlocked a drawer. He produced a wad of cash, counted out the money, and gave it to Thomas, a resentful frown on his face.

"I can't believe you would do this to your own flesh and blood. How can you call yourself an Elwood?"

"Believe me, I have no wish to. And don't you forget about mother. Leave word for me care of the bank. I'll be checking up on her."

After going to the kitchen to eat, Thomas retreated to his bedroom to get some rest. It would be another long night ride to Charleston.

He slept with a gun in his hand. His father would surely like nothing better than to see him dead to ensure that the past would forever remain buried in an empty coffin.

Waking around two in the morning, Thomas departed. As he rode, he fretted about Mosa. Those shackles fixed too tightly, rubbing her skin until it bled, and kept in the holding pen in the Mart like an animal. All the while wondering why Thomas had abandoned her.

When he arrived the following morning, the gates to Ryan's Mart were locked. A man told him the next sale was six days away. Thomas stopped people in the street to ask where Ryan lived. Getting an answer, he rode to his mansion in the best part of town.

"He ain't up yet," said the man answering the bell. "Did you want to wait?"

Thomas was cradling a warm cup of coffee in his hands when Ryan entered the room.

"I hear you have urgent business with me?"

"Yes, sir, I do," said Thomas rising to his feet. "I'm Thomas Elwood, son of George Elwood, owner of the Old Oaks Plantation."

"I've heard the name." Ryan didn't recognize Thomas from their encounter years ago, but then Thomas hadn't expected him to. "One of our slave girls was mistakenly sold to a passing trader a few days ago. I understand she may have been brought to your Mart for sale. My father has sent me to come get her back. We'll pay well over market price. Fifteen hundred dollars."

"Well, I can't deny that is an attractive offer. Meet me there in an hour and we'll see if I still have her."

"Still have her?"

"We had a sale yesterday. There's only a few left."

Thomas could see immediately they entered the windowless room at the Mart that she wasn't amongst the unfortunate souls chained to the walls.

"She's not here."

Ryan didn't attempt to hide his disappointment. He could have made a handsome profit.

"Who'd you sell her to?"

"That's confidential information. My information."

"I'll give you a hundred dollars for an answer."

"Two hundred."

"It's a deal."

"Name?"

"Mosa."

Ryan told him to wait outside his office. Thomas paced up and down until Ryan came back out.

"She was sold to a Mr. James Bulberry. He bought a few. Sent his overseer to transact the business. Plantation's near Macon, Georgia."

"How far is that?"

"Gotta be over two hundred miles."

"Which way did they go?"

"I can't rightly say. Ain't my business to ask such things. Now I don't mean to be discourteous but I've got work to do."

Standing in the street outside, Thomas considered what he could do next. If he could catch them, assuming they had taken the same route he would take, maybe he could cut a deal. That is if the overseer had permission to do so. However, since he had been given authority to make the purchase, it seemed likely he would have the power of sale also.

Yet by law Mosa was free, had been born free, and should never have been treated as a slave. The status of mixed race children was determined by their mother. The vast majority were born to women of color, impregnated by their white fathers. That way the law protected the interests of the slave owners, increasing the pool of available slave labor.

No one was likely to believe his assertion that she had come out of the same mother as he. His only hope was to buy Mosa back and protect her as her owner.

Thomas went to the bank to withdraw his savings. He didn't know how much he would have to pay for her. Two hundred dollars were already gone, and there would be the costs of getting to Macon and then up North. He also went to a bookstore to buy a map for his journey.

At least this time if he succeeded in his quest she would be legally his, not his father's. Northern states had succumbed to Southern pressure to return runaway slaves by agreeing to the passing of the Fugitive Slave Act in an attempt to hold the increasingly fractious Union together. Only Canada would have been entirely safe while others owned her. How ironic, he thought, that a country governed by the British Crown, seen less than a century ago as the tyrannical oppressor of the people, was now the only guaranteed place of freedom on the North American continent.

Although he didn't know it, Thomas would never catch up with them.

CHAPTER 18

Mosa and the five others bought the same day by Bulberry's overseer were already only a few hours from Macon. Yesterday they had been loaded onto a windowless freight wagon for Savannah and kept in it overnight. Early that morning they had been transferred to another boxcar hitched to a train bound for Georgia's heartland.

They had nothing to lie on and nowhere to answer the calls of nature. At first light, they had been given a crust of stale bread and a little water. Now it was past noon, and they were hungry and thirsty but unlikely to receive anything further until they reached their destination. The stench of their confined space made Mosa gag. She didn't recall ever feeling so sweaty or unclean.

She had no idea where she was headed. All Mosa knew was that it must be a long way, too far to escape from. Listlessly she rested her head against the wall, legs outstretched and arms hanging limply by her side. She didn't have the energy to cry.

Late afternoon, the train came to one final juddering halt. Eventually, the door to their boxcar slid open. It was the same unsympathetic man who had bought them and put them on the train.

"Out," was all he said.

They climbed down awkwardly in their shackles.

"May we please have some water?" asked Mosa, who by now had a splitting headache from dehydration.

"When we reach the plantation. I don't need y'all peeing in my nice clean cart. Now get on up there and stop complaining."

They bounced uncomfortably along the track for over an hour until they reached their journey's end. The plantation was many times the size of the two where Mosa had spent her life. Numerous slaves were toiling in the cotton fields.

Mosa tried to see a positive in her new situation. It was extremely difficult to find one. She hoped at least here she could be anonymous and avoid unwanted attention. She knew that Jefferson wasn't an isolated case.

The cart came to a stop at the slave quarters. Though the sun was going down the workers hadn't yet returned. Naked children ran around in the dirt. On this plantation, they didn't even give the young ones clothing. Finally, they were unshackled.

"Y'all be sleeping there for the time being," said the overseer indicating a building, if it could be called such. The wood was rotten and a past storm had ripped off part of the roof. There were no beds inside, just straw.

"Work starts at six tomorrow morning. I'll drop by with something you can cook in that fire pit. You can get water from the well. And don't even think about leaving. We'll catch you and brand your face with a big "R" for runaway. That'll be one letter you ignorant savages will learn to recognize if you're dumb enough to try."

Mosa was back in a living hell. Having spent time working in much better conditions as well as tasting the prospect of freedom, the fall into a pit of despair was like jumping off a cliff edge.

Not ever being able to ever read again seemed to Mosa the cruelest thing of all. How she had loved books. They had given wings to her imagination, allowing her to escape from reality. That night, she cried herself to sleep.

The following evening, she came back exhausted. Her hands were cut in several places, and the blisters from the day's labor had burst. Mosa's back ached from so many hours spent bent over the cotton. It had been a long time since she had worked outside, and here they demanded so much more than they had on the Brown plantation. If you missed your quota, you got a beating. She had only been let off as it was her first day.

Mosa couldn't envisage spending the next twenty, thirty, maybe even forty years living like this. She began to wonder if killing herself was the answer. Death would surely be a blessed release. Mosa didn't know how she would do it, but she just had to wait for the opportunity to present itself as at some point it surely would.

CHAPTER 19

It was three days later that Thomas arrived, not that Mosa knew that he had come looking for her.

He was surprised to see how modest the main house was given the significant area that the plantation encompassed. It was nothing like his father's home, merely a plain, unpainted wooden structure of only one story with a small veranda out front. Nor were there any gardens or neatly trimmed lawn surrounding it. Nothing to reflect the wealth this undertaking must undoubtedly generate.

He had passed the previous night at a hotel in town. After a few nights of sleeping rough, Thomas needed his clothes laundered and a bath. Arriving looking unkempt wouldn't help give the impression which he was hoping to convey. Nervous, he knocked on the door.

"Yes?" asked the slave who opened it. She was dressed as poorly as those he had seen working in the fields as he rode in.

"My name is Thomas Elwood, son of George Elwood of the Old Oaks Plantation in South Carolina. I wish to see the owner.

"He don't live here. This is Mr. Bennett's, the overseer's place. The owner lives in Macon. He's rarely here."

"Then I'll speak with Mr. Bennett."

She disappeared. As he waited outside, Thomas strained to see those working in the distance, trying to spot Mosa. It was useless; they were too far away for him to be able to discern any facial features.

"You wanted to see me, Thomas Elwood?" asked a surly voice.

The man looked irritated. Though it wasn't yet noon, Thomas could smell the alcohol on his breath, and the end of his nose was red and bulbous from a habit of too much drinking.

"Yes, sir, I did. I've traveled here from near Columbia in South Carolina where my family's plantation is situated. Pleased to make your acquaintance," he said offering his hand.

The overseer gave him a cursory handshake.

"I'll tell you whether I'm pleased to make yours when I know the reason why you have come here."

"There's been a terrible mistake. One of our slaves - Mosa's her name - was unintentionally sold to a passing trader, and I understand she has ended up in your care."

"The name rings a bell."

"We wish to buy her back. I appreciate the trouble that you have been put to bringing her here so I will pay you fifteen hundred dollars."

"Will you now. Why would anyone ride all the

way from South Carolina to pay over the odds for a nigger? I grant you she's not bad looking. Is she that good in the sack that you would pay so much? Maybe I should try her out myself."

Thomas bit his lip. How he would have loved to strike this odious character but he had to restrain himself. He was the supplicant here.

"As far as I'm concerned, she ain't for sale. If my answer ain't acceptable, you'll need to ask Mr. Bulberry himself. Now good day to you sir, and don't come back onto this property without his permission."

The house of Mr. Bulberry in town was in stark contrast to the one on the plantation. It shone in white. Columns all around it reached up to the roof like a latter-day Parthenon. Macon was replete with grand mansions, but this had to be one of the most imposing of all.

The slave greeting Thomas at the door was impeccably attired in a red coat and breeches down to his knees where they were met by long blue socks which appeared to be made of silk. It was as though he had been dressed to have the look of the Pre-Revolutionary era.

"Do you have an appointment, sir?"

"No."

"And the nature of your business?"

"It's something that I wish to discuss in private with Mr. Bulberry."

Thomas was told to return the following morning at eleven.

On arrival he was shown into the most palatial room he had ever entered. Two enormous chandeliers hung from the ceiling. The furnishings were equally elaborate and doubtless most valuable, imported at great expense from Europe.

A man with salt and pepper colored hair and a gray beard, and dressed in clothes that also looked expensive, got up to greet him and pointed to a gilded chair for him to sit on. Thomas explained the reason for his visit.

Despite the apparent cordiality of his welcome, Bulberry was immovable.

"I trust the judgment of my overseer, Mr. Elwood. If he says the answer is no, then that is my answer too."

"Two thousand," blurted out Thomas in desperation.

That would take every last cent to his name, but it would be worth it to obtain freedom for Mosa.

"I have already given you my decision."

"I beg you to reconsider, sir."

"Never beg, it is so unbecoming in a gentleman."

"She's my sister."

"And so might many other slave girls on your plantation be."

"No, my mother gave birth to her. By law, she is a free woman."

"And what proof do you bring with you of your assertion?"

"My word. On my life, I swear it is so."

"I have heard enough." He rang the bell on the table

beside him. "Abraham, please show Mr. Elwood out. Our meeting is over. And don't think of trying anything stupid, young man. Slave stealing remains a capital offense in Georgia."

CHAPTER 20

Thomas returned to his hotel. By the time he arrived there he had already determined what he must do. Time was of the essence. First, he took a quick nap. It would be a long night.

Early evening he set out. Thomas tied Shadow to a tree on the edge of the plantation and made his way toward the slave quarters, staying amongst the trees where he could, and crouching down and using bushes for cover in other spots.

He found a place in the undergrowth which gave him a clear view of the slave quarters. As it began to get dark, the workers returned. They were beyond weary, moving slowly, and with no energy left to talk to each other. Less than twelve hours to make some food, attend to any personal needs, and catch some sleep before it would it all start over again as it would, day after endless day, until death finally set them free.

Thomas saw Mosa. Her cheeks had become hollow, her eyes expressionless. The dress which she had once worn replaced by the coarse material that passed for clothing here. He saw her enter the most derelict of all the miserable dwellings. The others remained outside preparing food.

Later, when most had already gone inside to sleep, she came out again into the moonlight. She took a bucket from the well and walked away into the trees. Thomas followed and was about to reveal himself when she removed her dress to wash. He turned away. When he heard her put the dress back on, he emerged from the shadows.

"Mosa."

She jerked her head back in shock as if she had seen a ghost.

"It's me, Thomas. I've come to take you away."

"Oh, oh," was all she could manage, the sound exhaled in emotion.

He put his arms around her, and she lay her head on his chest. How he wanted to kiss her, tell her that he loved her, and wanted to marry her, but now he never could.

"I'm sorry it's taken me so long. I got mixed up in something, and by the time I got back to get you, my despicable father had sold you. But don't worry, I'm here now and we're getting away for good this time."

She looked up at him and ran her delicate fingers slowly down his cheek. A wet line ran down her face from beneath each of her eyes.

"Come, I have Shadow nearby."

They made their way off the plantation as fast as Thomas' withered leg would allow them.

"We're gonna make our way south-west to New Orleans and find a boat that's going North. They won't think we've stayed here in the South. They'll think we've gone North so they'll go looking for us in the wrong direction."

Thomas helped her up onto Shadow. Soon they would vanish into the night and be far away before that brutal overseer discovered Mosa had gone missing.

"Stop right there!"

Behind them, armed with rifles, stood Bennett and two of his men.

"Mr. Bulberry warned me you might be coming for her. Cuff them, boys."

They were led back onto the plantation.

"Take her back to the quarters. I'll deal with her tomorrow.

"Punish me, not her. This is my fault. I persuaded her to leave against her better judgment," pleaded Thomas.

"You'll be punished all right, have no fear. I'll take you into the Sheriff in the morning. You're a lucky man that Mr. Bulberry ordered me to follow due process. I would've shot you on the spot."

"Stay strong, Mosa. It's gonna be ok," called Thomas as they were separated. Her look of total fear made him loathe himself. He had failed her once again.

He spent a sleepless night in a wooden crate which was so small that he could neither stand or lie down, only crouch with his head near his knees and his back bent. But he knew the discomfort that he was experiencing would be nothing compared to the whipping Mosa would receive tomor-row.

Charged, Thomas was thrown in the town jail the next day. The day after he was brought before the judge.

"How do you plead. Guilty or not guilty?"

"Not guilty, your Honor."

"Your Honor we'll be pressing for the death pen-alty as provided for by statute should the defend-ant be convicted," said the prosecutor.

"I'm aware of the maximum penalty in this case, but it is rarely enforced these days for slave steal-ing."

"You are of course correct, Your Honor, but there has been a spate of slave stealing in these parts recently. We need to send a strong and clear mes-sage. If we don't, we'll have the abolitionists arriv-ing by the trainload fomenting trouble, inciting revolution and the murder of our citizens."

"I hear what you're saying. Should the defendant be found guilty, I may well be persuaded that such a course of action is required for the public good. Mr. Elwood, do you have a lawyer?"

"No, sir."

"Then I strongly advise you to engage one. Your life could depend on it."

CHAPTER 21

"What evidence can you produce, Mr. Elwood? I wouldn't want to risk my life on a jury taking my word for it."

The lawyer who the Sheriff had called in at Thomas' request was standing on the other side of the prison bars. Thomas recounted the family history.

"I assume your father wouldn't come to give evidence."

"No, he'd be happy if I were dead. How about the fact that he had my mother put in an asylum? That must prove it."

"Not necessarily. It's only your word again. Who apart from you can verify the facts? Without your father's confirmation, there's no guarantee that would be sufficient. The jurors are slave owners themselves. They truly hate white folk who try to spring a slave, believe me. Especially those from out of State."

"There's Maisie, the slave who was there at the birth."

"If she were white that would probably do it, but surely you know evidence from slaves isn't admissible in a court of law."

"Well, it looks like I'm done for. But I don't regret what I did. My only regret is Mosa spending her life here as a slave. In fact, anyone having to spend their life as a slave. It's wicked. How can we call ourselves Christians?"

"Stop will you. You give a jury any inkling of you thinking that way and they'll gladly lynch you themselves. You must keep such thoughts to yourself if you want to get out of the State of Georgia alive. Your time would be better spent thinking of who else might be able to help you."

"There is no one. No, wait. There is one person. My grandmother. My father accused her of telling me when I confronted him so she must know."

"That sounds promising. Will she come here to be a witness?"

"I doubt it. She lives in Charleston and must be very elderly and frail by now. I haven't seen her for years. We were never close."

"Would she swear to the facts you claim?"

"I can't say."

"A suitable deposition from her and your own account could well swing it. I'll leave you with this pen and paper for you to write to her. When you're done, I'll send your letter to a law firm I know of in Charleston. They will seek an appointment to talk with your grandmother. Meanwhile, I'll petition the judge for a postponement of the trial date to give us time."

"If I'm successful will the judge order the release of

Mosa?"

"That is a civil matter. I shall consider how that might be addressed, though we really must focus on saving you. If you hang, your sister's fate is sealed for eternity."

Thomas struggled to write to his grandmother. The woman was a virtual stranger to him. How could he appeal to her better nature, a side of her that he didn't recall ever having seen?

The wait for a response seemed interminable. Looking through the bars of the small opening at head height in his cell, Thomas could see a wooden platform and post. The noose which dangled from it swayed gently in the breeze. If his grandmother ignored him, one day soon he would be climbing up the steps onto that platform in the awful knowledge that Mosa would be spending the rest of her life as a slave.

At last, Thomas received word that his grandmother had agreed to meet the lawyer in Charleston, although he put it down to her natural curiosity rather than confirmation that she would assist.

A few days later a letter arrived from her. Thomas felt his hands shaking as he opened the envelope his lawyer had passed through the bars. Whatever words it contained could mean life or death for him, and freedom or enduring enslavement for Mosa. He wasn't feeling hopeful. He couldn't expect much from a woman who had never shown him any affection.

Dear Thomas

I am in receipt of your letter.

My initial instinct was to refuse to help as I consider that you have brought all this upon yourself by your impulsive and reckless behavior. However, I am cognizant of your point that you are now the heir to the plantation, which my late husband and your father have devoted their lives to.

Without you, the place will have to be sold. That would distress me greatly and although you are not well suited to the task, you are our only choice.

I am therefore minded to do as you ask in the belief that news of this torrid affair is unlikely to reach South Carolina. However, before I do so, I require your solemn promise on two matters.

First, you must never speak to anyone of your sister and, should she be freed, you will send her North and never utter a word about her or our family history. That includes not mentioning what happened to your mother.

Secondly, you shall return to the plantation and learn how to run it. You shall live there and agree to stay there for so long as you shall live. If you agree to my terms, I will also write to your father to smooth the way. I shall not mention your sister to him.

I await your response,

Your Grandmother

Thomas disliked her conditions but resigned himself to accepting them. With luck, Mosa would get to go North. He would miss her, but it was best that she establish her own independent life. Doing so here in the South would be so much more perilous. She would remain susceptible to being kidnapped by some unscrupulous trader. Taken off to another State and placed back into slavery, her claims that she was a free woman ignored.

Thomas had never wanted the plantation, but a career at the bank had not suited him either. Anyway, he was in no position to bargain. The new trial date was only a week and a half away. He wrote back to give his promise.

The morning that the trial was due to begin, his grandmother's sworn statement arrived. His lawyer secured a private audience with the judge and prosecutor, and the case was dropped. The judge even agreed an order that Mosa be recognized as a free woman.

Thomas rode out to Bulberry's place with Shadow attached to a cart to collect her. He felt as cheerful as the sunshine up above him. Bennett was expecting him.

"I knew I should've shot you when I had the chance. You may have pulled the wool over the judge's eyes, but not mine. She's waiting down at the quarters."

Thomas found Mosa sitting on a log, her back to him. She had become pitifully thin since being taken away from South Carolina. Not only were the bones on her shoulders prominent, but they seemed to sag with apathy and submission.

When Mosa heard him, she got up. He had expected to see joy as she turned around, but she showed none. She held one hand firmly against her left cheek.

"You're free, a free woman, Mosa," enthused Thomas as he got off his horse.

She didn't react.

"What's wrong, ain't you happy about that? I'm going to escort you to Charleston and find a boat to New York. You can start a new life."

"Like this?"

She removed her hand.

CHAPTER 22

Involuntarily, Thomas moved back a little.

"See, even you are horrified by me now."

The letter "R" had been branded into the flesh of her face. "R" for runaway, for having tried to flee.

"No, I'm not horrified just mad, mad at them. That they do such things to another human being. The sooner you're out of the South, the happier I'll be. Did Bennett tell you?"

"Tell me what?"

"Why you were free?"

"No."

Thomas reached out for her hands.

"Let's sit down. There's something I need to tell you. It will come as a shock."

They both sat down on the log. He coughed nervously.

"You're... you're my sister. We have the same mother and father."

"But how is that possible? You're white. I'm the result of some rape or illicit affair between a slave woman and a white man."

"That's what we all assumed. That night I came back to get you, Maisie told me the truth. She was there when you were born. She saw our mother give birth to you. Our father ordered Maisie to drown you in the river, but she took you to the Brown's plantation. It seems our great-great-grandmother was mixed race. My grandmother swore an oath to that effect. Maisie said the doctor at your birth said it can show up unexpectedly in a later generation."

Mosa looked away.

"Well, aren't you going to say something?"

"Say what? What am I supposed to say? That I fell in love with a man who I'm now told is my brother?"

"Yeah, it's awful hard, I know. I felt the same way about you, but we're just going to have to move on. We have no choice, Mosa. I'll always love you, but it can only be as a brother."

"You won't be coming with me then?"

"No, I'll be going back to the plantation. Don't worry though, I have almost three hundred dollars left to my name. You can have what remains to set you up once we've got back to Charleston and paid for your passage North."

Mosa remained crestfallen.

"Hey, I brought you a dress to wear. Why don't you go into the hut and swap those rags for it."

Thomas got the dress from the cart and handed it to her.

"You look wonderful," he said as she emerged after changing.

The dress was a striking purple with lace at the

collar and wrists. Mosa made no comment and didn't even smile.

"Come on. We ought to go. I don't want you spending another minute here."

They set off. Neither spoke. What more could they say? Their history dictated their future. A future of separation.

"Wait here. I'm gonna get you something. I don't think you need it, but if it makes you feel happier, it'll be worth it," said Thomas when they arrived in Macon.

He returned with a big white parasol.

"Just like the ladies use," he said, handing it to her. Mosa gave him a weak smile and held it so that it hid the left side of her face.

Back in Charleston some days later, they found a ship on the very day of their arrival which was going up the East Coast to New York that evening.

"Well, I guess this is goodbye," said Mosa as they stood by the vessel. The gloom of its shadow fell upon them, matching their mood.

"Only for a while. I'll come visit someday. Make sure you write. Often."

"I shall."

"You'd better get on. It's about to leave."

"Thank you, Thomas. You're the best brother a girl could have."

They hugged in the way that brothers and sisters do. Each was fighting against the urge to cry, each trying to be strong for the other.

Thomas watched the ship long after Mosa had

ceased waving and gone below deck, right until it had disappeared completely from view. She was gone. The one thing which he had really wanted in life, the one thing he could never have. Mosa had become a memory, not the happy future that he had imagined only a few weeks ago. Thomas didn't know when or if he would ever see her again. The exuberance of youth punctured beyond repair, he limped slowly back to the hotel where he would spend yet another lonely night.

CHAPTER 23

The first night of the voyage a storm hit. As the ship pitched in the maelstrom, Mosa thought of those who once had crossed this ocean on their way to North America, not as passengers but as human cargo. How terrifying it must have been for them, going to where they knew not, knowing only one thing for certain, that they would never see their loved ones again. When Mosa had been sold, she had believed that her life would take the same course.

With stops along the way, it was over four long days to New York. As the only mixed race person on board, she ate alone and spent most of her time shut in her tiny cabin. But Mosa didn't mind that. She had time to think and books to read once more. Thomas had bought her some for the journey. It felt such a luxury to hold them in her hands and see the printed word, something she had thought that she would never do again during those dark days in Georgia.

The shock of discovering that she was Thomas' sister had begun to subside. She had a past now. Although Mosa would never have a mother and a father who would know her for who she was, she knew where she came from, and she had a brother who cared. A brother who had risked his life for her. For the first time in her life, Mosa felt a whole person. She had an identity, one which had caused rejection and pain, but she finally had an answer to the question which had plagued her since childhood. Who was she?

That she and Thomas couldn't be together hurt, but in time that feeling would end. The hurt of a lifetime spent on Bulberry's plantation would never have ended. Her future was hers, a book yet to be written. One that she, not some unfeeling overseer, could write. She was free and that, despite all which had happened to her, was still a wonderful thing.

On arrival, Mosa was astounded by the size of the city that emerged out of an early morning fog. Buildings crammed together, streets thronging with people. She had never imagined that such a place could exist.

To hide her past, she had taken to wearing a head wrap, tied so it covered part of her cheeks and the indelible "R". She had cried when she had looked at her face in the small mirror which hung on her cabin wall. Though she had felt her branding so many times, running her fingers around its outline, that was the first time that she had ever got to see it in all its ugliness; pink flesh, cracked and rough to the touch. But here in New York nobody gave Mosa a second glance. Everyone was too busy to take any notice of a newcomer.

Mosa began a search for work and somewhere to live. Asking for a room to rent with the money Thomas had given her, she found that this land of freedom wasn't all she had expected it to be. Repeatedly rebuffed, one answer she got was more helpful than most.

"I only rent to white folk. You're in the wrong part of town. You need to go to Greenwich where the Negroes live."

Taking the advice, Mosa found a room in the black part of town. When she mentioned her interest in teaching, the owner suggested that she should inquire at the Colored Orphan Asylum.

"They've got over two hundred kids there. They're always looking for help."

Arriving for her interview, Mosa was astonished to see the building. She had expected something ramshackle. It was, however, a magnificent structure; a four-story building with little towers and sloping roofs in the style of a French chateau standing amongst trees and surrounded by lawn. In the South, only plantation owner's houses were so extravagant. Financed by charitable donations from white patrons, it was a well-equipped institution.

They were glad to hire Mosa. She soon became firm friends with Martha, another teacher working there, who had fled from Virginia a few years earlier.

When not working, Mosa would walk the streets

of New York and marvel at how it buzzed with activity. She would stop and stare longingly at the fine dresses displayed in shop windows. Mosa still had some money left from what Thomas had given her, but decided she should keep that as a buffer, something to fall back on just in case. Now she had a job, it wouldn't be long until she could afford to buy some new clothes.

"You should come with me this evening," said Martha one late September day. "I'm going to an election rally for Mr. Lincoln. He's our best chance of ending slavery. He opposes its extension into the New Territories out West. In time, he may come to oppose it in the South as well."

"Can colored folk vote up here?"

"No, they had a referendum earlier this year to grant universal suffrage in the State to men over twenty-one, but it was defeated. Only our men folk with sufficient wealth get to vote, and there ain't many of them. But I still want to support the cause."

"OK, I'll come."

Mosa and Martha strolled arm in arm to the venue. Though she had been in New York for over a month now, Mosa still couldn't help smiling as she went around. She was free, free to walk about and be her own person, not just a thing to be used and abused.

There was much poverty on show. Many people lived and died on the streets, but Mosa concluded she would rather die free than live enslaved.

A noisy crowd was milling around the entrance to the hall when they arrived, shouting anti-Lincoln slogans.

"Let's slip in the side entrance," said Martha.

"Who were they?"

"Democrat supporters who believe Lincoln's agenda will tear the country apart."

Inside, man after man took to the podium. Soon Mosa's enthusiasm for the event waned. It seemed unending. Try as she might, she could concentrate no longer.

"Kinda long, huh?"

Mosa turned to her side. A young man with eyes that seemed to dance and a smile that took up almost the entire width of his face, stood next to her.

"Lloyd Jenkins at your service, ma'am."

"Mosa. Mosa Elwood."

It still felt awkward to say Elwood. A last name had never been needed on the plantation, albeit if one was required, slaves were generally referred to by their owner's last name. Though Mosa was an Elwood by blood, the name made her uncomfortable. It wasn't one that gave her pride when she thought of what the family stood for.

"Pleased to make your acquaintance. You appear to have an interest in politics which is, if I may say so, unusual in young ladies."

"I was a slave once so maybe it's not that surprising to want to hear about those who may end it."

"Indeed. Please accept my apologies if I have

caused offense."

"No need sir. When you have lived the life which I have, you would never take offense at anything so trivial."

"I'm an abolitionist. Some of them disown Lincoln because he won't commit to abolishing slavery, but he's the only candidate who might go down that road so I'll be voting for him this November. They say if he wins, the South could secede and that will lead to war."

"I too have heard such talk. The thought of all the killing that would come from a war saddens me, although I have only ever met one white Southern man who didn't support slavery. I don't see them ever agreeing to abandon it voluntarily."

"Exactly. War may be the only path to freedom for all. Have you been in the city long?"

"A few weeks. I work at the Colored Orphan Asylum. I teach them to read and write."

"That is an admirable profession. I fear my vocation is much less commendable."

"And what might that be?"

"I'm an engineer involved in the construction of Central Park."

"Really. I've heard many had to be moved off their land to accommodate it. Colored folk who had established a fully functioning village with churches and schools."

"Seneca Village. I'm afraid so, though they were compensated."

"Maybe the landowners were, not those who

rented their homes. They had established a life for themselves there. A whole community destroyed. If the residents had been white, I dare say a different location would have been chosen for the park."

"Sometimes relocation is sadly unavoidable. New York's population has quadrupled these past thirty years. You will have noticed how overcrowded it is. Somewhere had to be found to give the people some green space."

"Yes, I can see that. In South Carolina, where I'm from, there's plenty of space. Only problem is you can't just wander and enjoy it, unless of course by accident of birth you're born white like yourself."

"That must have been hard to endure. I hope you won't consider me too bold for asking but I was wondering whether you might consider taking a stroll with me on Sunday afternoon?"

Mosa touched the side of the dark blue head wrap she wore. How could she ever get close to a man? If she removed it, that would be the end of any relationship. Why start something that would only cause heartache.

"That's most kind but I'm unable to accept. I have a prior engagement. It's been a pleasure to meet you, but I must rejoin my friend. She'll be wanting to leave now. Goodbye, Mr. Jenkins."

"What'd you do that for?" asked Martha who had overheard the last part of the conversation.

"I don't need a man to complete me."

"I know that but that don't mean it won't make

you happier."

"I'm tired. Thanks for bringing me. I'll see you in the morning."

"OK. Goodnight."

Mosa lay in bed, unable to sleep. From outside, came the occasional shouts of drunks. Tonight she felt so alone. She ran her fingers over her scar as she had done countless times. Free she may be, but the story of her past would forever be written across her face for all to see, and her disfigurement would impact her future. It already had.

This city wasn't home. Maybe home was somewhere Mosa would never find. Perhaps loneliness was to be her destiny, the price of her freedom. After all, she had been lonely nearly her entire life. The man who had ended her solitude for a short while was hundreds of miles away. Mosa hugged her pillow tight.

Come morning she felt better. The start of a new day always had that effect. Mosa enjoyed her job and loved watching the children progress. They were getting the best chance that they could to be able to make something of their lives, not like those in South Carolina. There their future had been written the day they were born, and it didn't involve an education.

On Friday, Mosa received a delivery in class. She blushed at the sight of the flowers. Excited chatter broke out amongst the boys and girls.

"Be quiet children and get on with your work. I'll be back momentarily."

Mosa walked hurriedly out of the room to the kitchen to find a vase and some water. Relieved that cook was elsewhere, she put the flowers on the table and read the card.

Whatever blemish you may be hiding, nothing could outshine your beauty. I'll be outside the Orphanage at 3 pm Sunday should you wish to take a walk with me. Yours respectfully, Lloyd Jenkins.

Mosa's heart fluttered. Maybe Martha was right.

CHAPTER 24

An uneasy truce existed at Old Oaks Plantation. Not long after Mosa's departure for New York, Thomas had once again stood before his father seated at his desk. But that no longer bothered Thomas. The balance of power had changed. The man could no longer be a tyrant toward his son.

"Your grandmother's written to me. I understand you've agreed to come learn how to run this place and keep your mouth firmly closed."

"And mother?"

"She's being well cared for in Charleston. You're free to go visit."

"I shall."

"O'Connell, my new overseer, will be teaching you most things."

"What happened to the other one?"

"He got drunk too often. I had to fire him. By the way, it would be better if you don't dine with us. Your presence here makes Emma uncomfortable."

"That's fine by me."

The arrangement suited Thomas perfectly. He had no wish to spend any more time in his father's company than was absolutely necessary.

"I suppose you're hoping that renegade Lincoln gets elected this fall."

"I believe in the Union if that's what you mean."

"Well take my word for it, if he wins he'll destroy the Union. Those Yankees are so goddamn sanctimonious, telling us how to live our lives. I know you don't believe in slavery, but at least down here the Negro has a roof over his head and food in his stomach. Freedom comes at a price in the North. There's plenty of them starving to death up there. If they can't find work, they're done for. And if you vote to free them in the South, you better sleep with a loaded gun in your hand because they'll want revenge. We'll be driven off our land. Become outcasts in our own country."

As he rode around the plantation, Thomas came across Maisie.

"Hello, Maisie. How are you keeping?"

"Well enough. Thank you for keeping your word. It sure was sad that your daddy sold Mosa."

"Can you give me your word, Maisie, to take another secret to the grave if I tell you something?"

"Will it get me into trouble?"

"No."

"Then I give you my word."

"Mosa's free and safe up North."

"Praise the Lord. I'm so happy for her, but I shall never tell a soul. May I ask you a question?"

"Try me. I won't answer it if I don't want to."

"Did you...did you open the grave?"

"You were right. I shouldn't have. Well, good day

to you now."

He nudged Shadow with his boot and trotted away to find O'Connell. Thomas and O'Connell took an immediate mutual dislike to each other. Thomas saw in him a man of ignorance and prejudice. O'Connell no doubt viewed Thomas as weak and naive.

"Your father's been way too generous, lets them work at their speed. The Negro is like a mule, naturally lazy. They'll cheat you if you let them."

"I don't regard these people as animals, Mr. O'Connell. Have you ever spent a day in their shoes, working in the fields as they do? If you had, I think it might change your opinion."

"Your father said you were an idealist, but idealism won't keep this place together or keep them fed and sheltered."

"Neither will punishment."

Thomas departed deliberately quickly, letting Shadow come within an inch of the man before changing course. O'Connell cursed under his breath as he was forced to move out of the way.

Thomas felt as if there were a pressure valve inside him waiting to explode. A stress he couldn't shake off. His grandmother had exacted a high price. He didn't know how long he could live here under his father's roof.

Only when a letter arrived from Mosa did his mood improve. She sounded fulfilled which lifted his spirits. How he would find his own fulfillment in this oppressive environment, he didn't know.

CHAPTER 25

Lloyd had been about to leave when Mosa arrived. "I thought you weren't going to come."

"I wasn't. I changed my mind at the last minute."

"A woman's prerogative."

"Exactly."

She was wearing the same gray dress which she had worn the evening they had met, but today she had a red cape around her shoulders to keep out the chill of an usually cold day. Mosa had a prettier dress but had decided she didn't want to come in that for their first meeting. Lloyd might take it as a sign that she was keen.

"I hope you didn't mind my message. I know you must have suffered. Sufferings which I can only guess at."

"Can we not talk about that today. I want to think about something else, something hopeful."

"Then may I suggest that I show you the work going on to create Central Park. It'll put New York on the map as a world city like London and Paris which already have their own parks. Ours will be the biggest and best."

"Take me there. It sounds impressive."

He showed her the work already completed and explained what was to come.

"This park will be the City's lungs. A place where anyone, rich or poor, can come regardless of color."

"If they can get here. It's close to where the wealthy live, and an awful long walk from where most of the poor live. How come you got involved in the cause, Mr. Jenkins?"

"Please call me Lloyd. I believe in the dignity of everyone. Our Declaration of Independence says all men are created equal, not only white men. If war comes, I intend to join the army and fight for freedom."

"Those are noble ideals, Lloyd."

"What life will we have lived if we aren't willing to try and make a difference, Mosa. May I call you Mosa?"

"You already have. I sense you're a man who does what he wants and gets what he wants."

"Sometimes."

"Well, I really must be going now. It's been a fascinating afternoon."

"Might we meet again next Sunday?"

"Yes, we might."

And they did, and they met regularly after that.

Fall was now well underway. It was a windy day. Red and yellow leaves fell from the trees like confetti. Lloyd slipped his hand into hers as they walked along. Mosa didn't resist at first but then dropped his and moved away.

"I like you Lloyd but we can't do this."

"Why?"

"Look at our skin. We aren't the same you and I."

"What does that matter? It's not unlawful in the State of New York."

"Not unlawful maybe but think about how we'd be shunned by your family, your friends, by society. There might be no slavery here but there's a separation, a definite line you don't cross. And I've spent my life being rejected because I'm neither one color or another. I don't want to inflict that on anyone else."

"I don't care, Mosa. You're the best thing that's ever happened to me. We'll leave New York, go somewhere else if need be. Canada. The British are much more open-minded about such things."

"Color's not the only reason. Watch."

Mosa unwound her head wrap, revealing all of her face to him for the first time. To her, it was as if she were undressing until she was naked, laying bare her vulnerability and insecurity. Lloyd gently placed his fingers on her scar.

"Does it still hurt?"

"Not physically, but mentally it hurts. Every day."

"Well, you're still the most beautiful woman in the world to me."

He leaned forward to kiss her. She didn't move away this time.

A couple of weeks later Lloyd broke into a run when he saw Mosa.

"He's done it!" he said picking her up at the waist

and twirling her around.

"Put me down, will you. I know he's done it, I don't live on the moon."

"Why aren't you ecstatic then?"

"Of course I'm pleased Lincoln's been elected, but a lot of people are probably going to die. Maybe even you. It scares me, Lloyd."

"Will you wait for me, Mosa?"

"But you ain't had to go anywhere yet. Maybe there'll be a miracle and there'll be no war."

"I've enlisted. I want to be trained and ready to go."

"Oh."

"I'd ask you to marry me but I think that would be wrong. Just in case."

"You know what my answer would be."

She smiled mischievously.

"That's all I need to know."

"When do you leave?"

"The day after tomorrow."

"The day after tomorrow? But that's so quick."

"If there's a war, it'll be over in twelve months. They've only got cotton fields. We've got factories producing what's needed to beat them. I bet I'll be home for next Christmas. We can have a winter wedding. You can wear fur. You'll be prettier than a Christmas tree."

That made Mosa laugh.

"I've been compared to many things, but a tree's a first." The moment of levity was brief. "I knew another kind man once. I loved him. I still do, in a different way. But we could never marry. Losing him hurt. I don't want to lose the man I love again."

"You won't. I promise."

"A promise is easily made and easily broken. Don't make one that you don't know you can keep."

CHAPTER 26

Thomas had never felt as though he belonged in South Carolina. It represented a future he didn't subscribe to. It was the epitome of a slave state. Almost half of the white population had at least one. There was no way that they were ever going to agree to relinquish slavery. It gave them a comfortable life. They saw nothing wrong in enslaving others to enrich themselves. After all, had not these people lived as godless savages in Africa? Their owners felt righteous that they had, in their opinion, civilised them. Southerners had convinced themselves that Northerners wanted to destroy the South's economy and way of life to make her subservient and powerless, and were using the existence of slavery as a convenient excuse to do so.

A few days after the Presidential election, the State Legislature in Columbia passed a resolution calling the election of Lincoln as President of the United States a hostile act. The Legislature was controlled by the self-interested landowners. Only those with at least five hundred acres of land and not less than ten slaves as well as one hundred and fifty pounds sterling, the world's then-dominant currency, were eligible to sit.

They stated their intention to secede from the United States. And in December 1860 they did, declaring themselves the Palmetto Republic. Down came the Stars and Stripes and up went a new flag, blue with a dwarf white palm tree and crescent moon. They called on the other slaveholding states to join them.

"A great day for us all," enthused George Elwood as Jeremiah left the drawing room having erected the Christmas tree. George was impervious to the fact that it was far from a great day for the state's black population for whom freedom seemed to have moved even further out of reach.

"I believe it's the beginning of the end for your way of life," said Thomas.

"You should be careful what you say from now on. You'll be branded a traitor. Keep your thoughts to yourself if you want to live. You need to join up. Both of Gregory Brown's sons have already done so."

"With a leg like mine?"

"You can still ride a horse."

"I'm not fighting."

"If Jefferson were here, he would enlist."

"Well, I'm not Jefferson."

"No, you're a coward as well as a cripple," said his father, grabbing the sleeve of Thomas' jacket as he went to go.

"Get off me."

Thomas swung his arm back in anger, hitting his father in the face. The force of the blow knocked him backward, and he lost his balance and fell onto the floor.

Thomas looked at him lying there, a man he despised, yet a man whose blood ran through his veins. An inescapable part of who Thomas was. He was seized by an overwhelming need to change his life. He could no longer keep his word to his grandmother and stay here. He had to leave. Go North for his sanity.

George Elwood made no attempt to stand back up. Instead, he clutched at his chest and began writhing in agony.

"I'm in pain. Get help." Thomas didn't react. "Help me, damn you."

But Thomas called no one and offered no assistance. Impassively, he stood there and watched his father die.

Thomas and Emma exchanged no words with each other at the funeral which took place three days after Christmas. She left the following morning, returning to family in Charleston. Thomas found himself master of the plantation. Master of a place that he had never wanted to be master of.

If he could, he would have freed the slaves and gone North, but he couldn't liberate them. The law didn't allow it. And if he sold the property, they would be in the hands of someone who would likely care very little about what happened to them. Once again, he felt he had no choice.

He had to stay. It was his duty. To try and make amends for all that had been perpetrated in the name of his family.

Now in charge, he could introduce changes. He called O'Connell to the house.

"Mr. O'Connell, I don't want any more whippings on my land."

"Then how do you expect to control them?"

"I intend to gain their respect."

"You won't do that without the whip. Fear breeds respect."

"You are free to leave if you don't like my methods."

O'Connell muttered something that he hadn't the courage to say out loud. Thomas ignored it.

"Do you understand my order?"

The man gave a barely perceptible nod.

"Good. You may leave now."

O'Connell bit his tongue. He needed this job, even if it meant working for a nigger lover.

Thomas bought new clothes for the slaves, instituted better food rations, and shortened working hours. He was free to talk with them again, just like when he was younger before his father had forbidden it.

In April 1861, he went down to Charleston to visit his mother. She was unchanged but he took comfort from the much-improved care that she now received. He booked a hotel room. His days of riding through the night were over.

Early the next morning, Thomas was woken by

the sustained sound of firing. He dressed quickly and ran downstairs to investigate.

"It's started," said the owner. "Our boys are attacking Fort Sumter out in the harbor. The Yankee soldiers retreated there like rats down a drain pipe after we seceded. We can't leave them there. If they remain in control of the fort, their navy would be able to get right into the harbor and attack us."

Thomas rode down to the waterfront to witness history in the making. Thick smoke rose from the walls of the fort into the sky, obscuring the early morning sun. Bystanders cheered, but not Thomas. This was the point of no return. There was no going back. The battle was still raging when he left Charleston to return home. It raged for over thirty hours until the Union soldiers surrendered.

The Civil War had begun. Ahead lay death and destruction on a scale no one could yet imagine. American deaths would be greater than any other war the country has been involved in before or since.

CHAPTER 27

When news of the attack reached New York, there was a clamor for action.

"Those Southerners finally went too far this time. War is what they want and war is what they're gonna get," said Martha. "You dun heard from Lloyd recently?"

"He writes when he can," replied Mosa, hiding her disappointment at how infrequently he did so.

Mosa didn't hear from him for another two months. When the letter came, it wasn't the romantic one that she had been expecting.

Dear Mosa,

I hope all is well with you.

I have been moved to Washington. Now the war has begun, it is likely to become the primary target of the Confederacy, sitting as it does on the front line between North and South.

They say if the city were to fall that could be the end of the war so its defense has assumed the utmost importance.

My engineering skills are being tested to the limit in assisting with the building of new fortifications to protect our capital. We are constructing forts on the high ground, and artillery is positioned in the spaces in between.

Washington is overflowing with people, especially fugitive slaves seeking freedom. The humidity is much worse than New York. It is a place of flies, mosquitoes, and bad smells.

I had the greatest honor yesterday. Mr. Lincoln himself came to inspect our work. He stopped to speak to me, asking why I had joined the army.

When I told him because I believed in liberty for all, he said that day would surely come. I'm of the opinion that he wants slavery ended in all parts of the nation and is only waiting for the right moment to say so.

I must close now. I have no more paper and it is late. I should get some rest before another busy day.

Your Lloyd

Although relieved to hear from him again, doubts began to toy with Mosa. Out of sight, out of mind. His letter was matter of fact, not intimate at all.

After this last one, his letters ceased entirely. Not knowing if he were dead or had been taken prisoner was difficult to cope with. Mosa threw herself into her work, grateful she had employment that she loved and which filled her days leaving less time to worry about what had become of Lloyd.

Letters from Thomas were still getting through. Life had become a struggle even for the privileged landowners.

The South had self-imposed a ban on cotton exports hoping that Great Britain, its major customer, once deprived of supplies would then join the war on the side of the South. However, that strategy had failed. Britain had turned instead to Egypt and India for the cotton which she needed. A bad harvest at home had also made Britain reliant on grain imports from the North. King Cotton trumped by King Grain. And the British public were opposed to the institution of slavery, so there was no support for taking up arms to help the South.

The Union navy mounted a blockade to preempt any change of mind the South might have about not selling cotton, and also to prevent supplies getting through to the Confederacy. There were blockade runners who managed to get some cotton out, but they could only take a limited quantity and the price to do so was high.

Income is at an all-time low, wrote Thomas. *Some of the slaves have fled to join the Union army. I don't begrudge them, though they risk their lives in getting North. Stories are rife of angry Southerners attacking slaves who leave plantations, blaming them rather than themselves for our sorry state of affairs.*

Those who have remained work hard to help me grow the cotton which we may never sell. In the evenings, we all toil together growing vegetables and tending hogs. My biggest concern is to ensure that I can feed everybody.

Still, despite these challenging times, I am happier than I have been in some while. I enjoy the outdoor life and the camaraderie of all pulling together in a com-

mon purpose.

I had to let O'Connell go. He never agreed with my methods.

Even if I had the money to hire a replacement, I doubt I would find one. The draft has taken most able-bodied white men away to fight. Although, as always, it is the poorest who must go. This time

for the right of the wealthy to own slaves. Those with money have been able to avoid the draft, including myself as I satisfy the exemption of having over twenty slaves to look after.

Once this war is over and hopefully with a Northern victory, it may finally be possible for me to leave here. I should like to travel to Europe.

Have you any more news from Lloyd? Do write soon.

I am glad that you are in New York and out of harm's way.

With love,

Thomas

Mosa sighed. She did miss the place she was from if not its way of life. Perhaps when this war was over she could return for a visit or Thomas could visit New York on his way to Europe.

Many months passed. News of victories and setbacks filtered through from time to time. Lloyd's belief that the war would be over in a year proved ill-founded.

As Mosa walked to work one morning in July 1863, a man deliberately bumped into her on the street. The force of it almost knocked her over.

"Your kind should get back South," he shouted.

"We don't want hordes of niggers coming up to steal our work when this war's over."

Mosa didn't respond. She carried on, head down, hoping not to invite any more attention to herself.

"What's the matter?" asked Martha when Mosa arrived at work visibly shaken.

"A man yelled at me in the street. Told me to go back South. Said we were coming to steal their jobs."

"Oh dear. Tensions were already high since Lincoln announced the draft. I heard the Democratic Party is winding folk up, saying all our brothers and sisters down South will soon be here taking their jobs for less pay. The Irish immigrants are particularly susceptible to their rabble-rousing. They get called the "Blacks of Europe". They are at the bottom of society, only just above our own people. The politicians make us the scapegoats to get their votes.

"Matron says there's been rioting in parts of the city. The army's off fighting the war and many of the police, who are Irish themselves, are turning a blind eye. The best thing we can do is stay inside until it's blown over. I'll get a bed made up for you so you don't have to walk home tonight."

"Thanks, Martha. I appreciate that."

The following afternoon as the children sat at their desks writing, Mosa stood by her table at the front of the classroom re-reading the letter from Thomas. Shouting from outside interrupted her.

"What's that Miss?" asked one of the children.

"It's nothing to worry about, Benjamin. Get on with your work."

The shouts became louder and more threatening. Mosa went over to look out of the window. Armed with clubs and other weapons, an angry mob had gathered in front of the orphanage.

One man spotted Mosa and hurled a brick toward her, breaking the glass. She let out an involuntary scream. Terrified children looked at her for reassurance. Then came the noise of the entrance door to the building being battered until it opened.

"It'll be all right children. I want you to hide under your desks and not come out unless I tell you to. Daniel and Jobe, come over here and help me push this bookcase against the door.

"Good, now we'll push my desk in front of it to stop it toppling over."

By now the rabble was rampaging through the corridors like an invading army.

"Look at what they got. More than we've ever had that's for damn sure. All this food and bedding," cried one.

"Grab all you can. Why should niggers have all this?" called another. "When we're done, we'll set the place on fire."

Fire. The word cut through Mosa like a knife. The children were trapped in this classroom on the second floor. She could see their frightened eyes looking at her from under the desks as if vulnerable cubs hidden in a den who would be killed if discovered.

The sound of heavy footfalls outside ended but quiet proved to be no friend. Smoke began seeping through the gaps between the door to the classroom and the door frame. She would have to risk it. The children would be burned alive if they remained here.

"Boys, help me move the furniture back from the door."

Once the door was accessible again, Mosa addressed the class.

"Right children, I want you to come out. You're going to follow me calmly down the staircase, holding hands, two by two. Then we're gonna go outside and keep walking until I tell you to stop. No one is to say a word. Keep your heads down and don't look at nobody."

Flames were already working their way toward them as they filed out and down the stairs. Children from the other classes were also making their way out. Staff carried the sick from the hospital room who were too ill to walk.

Outside, the mob pulled back a little to let them pass, watching in an ominous silence. Undecided about their next move, their mood remained ugly.

"Remember what I said children. Heads down and keep walking."

Mosa glanced behind. The whole building was alight now. Flames leaped out of the window of her classroom. She suppressed her urge to confront the rioters and scold them for attacking defenseless orphans but she couldn't, that would be to risk the children's lives, not just her own.

So she too looked down as she walked, though she could feel the eyes of every rioter were fixed upon them. Scared, Mosa fought hard not to show it. She had to remain composed for the children. If any of them wavered, the crowd would surely sense that, and descend on them like a pack of wolves on a wounded animal.

One of the mob took pity on them and shouted out:

"If there is a man among you with a heart within him come and help these poor children."

Hearing the sound of scuffling, Mosa looked up. The crowd had set upon him.

"Hurry children, hurry," she urged.

How long would it be until energized by an attack on one of their own, the rioters would turn on the orphans. Mercifully, they didn't.

Matron led the long line of newly homeless to the police station on Thirty-Fifth Street. There they had to stay in cramped conditions for three days until the rioting was ended by troops sent from the recently fought Battle of Gettysburg.

Commonly known as the New York Draft Riots, they were the most serious civil insurrection the country had experienced. Afterward, most of the black population left Manhattan, many choosing Brooklyn as a safer spot to live. The outcome was a Confederate victory in all but name.

The orphans were taken to Blackwell's Island,

now known as Roosevelt Island, between Manhattan and Queens. It was an unsavory place. The location for a lunatic asylum, workhouse, and penitentiary; a far cry from their previous neighborhood.

CHAPTER 28

"Will we be safe here, Miss?" asked Nina, one of the girls in her class, when they arrived.

"We sure will, honey," answered Mosa. Although once the children were asleep that first night on Blackwell's Island, the latest news didn't comfort her.

"They say that they even attacked two white women married to colored men as well as stringing up plenty of colored folk," Martha told her as they sat that evening outside the grimy building which would now be the orphanage.

"It's so sad. So sad we have to define ourselves by color. I sometimes wonder what difference this war is really gonna make."

"I don't know but when Lloyd comes home, you two need to think seriously about where you'll live. New York is too dangerous for an interracial couple after what has happened here."

"I agree," said Mosa, wondering if he ever would come home. "All that talk of how Lincoln's Emancipation Declaration would change things. It hasn't. It's just a declaration by one man."

"It was a calculated move to get support from

abolitionists and colored folk, especially in the South. He knew he'd face a backlash, but he must have determined it would help the war effort more than hinder it."

"Exactly. If he wins the slaves in the South will be freed in law, but freeing people's minds of prejudice and changing their attitudes, that's going to take generations. I often wish I'd been born a hundred years in the future when this is all ancient history. When the world we live in is no longer bothered by what color you happen to be."

"That's a nice thought," said Martha. "But if politicians are still behaving like they are today, goading people into hating others to get themselves elected, telling them they're the cause of their problems, it might not be much different than it is today. Slavery might end but that don't mean they won't find other ways to keep us down."

"I hope you're wrong about that."

"Me too."

"Just look at this place, Martha. Don't it make you wanna cry for the children. It's dirty and rat infested, nothing like they had before. I can't understand why they targeted us, an orphanage of all places."

"Matron says the police told her that they were angry with our white benefactors for funding us instead of their own kind. I heard talk they're planning to move us back to Manhattan in a few months, but it ain't gonna be like the beautiful place we had. Still, we all got out alive which is a blessing we must be thankful for."

Mosa wrote to Thomas to tell him of her new address. Not wishing to alarm him, she downplayed events.

Three weeks later she received a letter back from South Carolina. However, it wasn't handwriting which she recognized. Come evening, she took it outside and sat down on the ground to open it.

Dear Miss Elwood,

It is with great regret that I write to inform you of the untimely death of Mr. Thomas Elwood who passed on July 25th. Please accept my condolences for your loss.

My law firm are the executors of his last will and testament.

I am writing to inform you that you are the sole beneficiary of his entire estate.

You can assume possession of his assets or require them to be sold. The Plantation, which is by far the most valuable asset, would be likely to fetch only a modest sum given current circumstances.

May I please ask you to get in touch at your convenience to advise what you wish us to do.

Yours truly

Matthias Coburg

Attorney at Law

Mosa slumped down onto the ground sobbing. Thomas, her kind and generous brother, was dead. The man who had taught her to read and write, and who had saved her on more than one occasion. Now he would never get to go to Europe or find the love that he so richly deserved.

Not wanting anyone to see her in such distress, Mosa got up. She needed time alone. She hurried off, seeking privacy for her grief.

Shouting from the nearby lunatic asylum resonated in the hot summer air. She continued on until reaching the end of the island, finding a secluded spot under a tree.

When her tears stopped flowing, Mosa sat and thought. She stayed there beyond dark, into the night, all night.

As the sun rose, Mosa walked back toward the orphanage. Martha came running when she saw her, throwing her arms around her.

"Mosa, you're alive. We've all been so worried about you. Is it Lloyd?" she asked, noticing the agony of last night still etched upon Mosa's face.

"No. It's my brother."

"Brother? I never knew you had one." Mosa choked back fresh tears. "You poor thing. Has he been killed fighting?"

"I don't know. I just got a letter from his lawyers saying he's dead. They didn't say how."

"His lawyers? Your brother has lawyers?"

"Yes, he owns a plantation in South Carolina. He's left it all to me."

Martha was rendered speechless for several seconds.

"Oh Lord, what shall you do?"

"I was up all night thinking about that. I must go back."

"Go back? You can't, it's too dangerous."

"I owe it to him, to them. The folk forced to work there. What'll become of them if the place isn't kept going? Where will they go? What will they live on? They could starve. And if I sell it, who knows what kind of monster will become their new owner. You've seen what white people will do to us."

"You can't take on everybody's burden, Mosa. We need you here."

"You'll all manage just fine without me but they won't. My mind's made up. There's no changing it."

Martha could see by the look of determination on Mosa's face that there was no point trying to dissuade her.

"What if Lloyd writes?"

"I'll leave you my address. I need to speak to Matron and then go pack."

"I'll miss you so much, Mosa."

"And me you but I have to do this. I couldn't live with myself if I didn't."

"I understand. Come, I'll help you get ready."

Martha took her arm and they went inside.

CHAPTER 29

Mosa took a train South as far as she could. When the service ended with a squealing of brakes, she got off and began to walk.

Smoke floated along the horizon from a battle raging in the distance, a line which she would need to cross. Recent rainfall had turned the tracks into a quagmire. It wasn't long until her boots and the lower half of her dress were caked in mud.

In the fields, black men were collecting bodies and loading them onto stretchers. Two came toward her, one carrying the front, the other holding the back. Mosa could see boots and legs dangling over the side closest to her, the corpses laid across the stretcher so more could be carried at a time.

As they came closer, she recoiled in horror. The other side of the stretcher was now visible to her. Hanging out of tattered uniforms were skulls. The laborers were collecting the remnants of another battle fought some time ago. Soldiers whose bodies had become skeletons, lying dead and unclaimed, their flesh food for birds and rodents.

Mosa felt as though she were walking toward the gates of hell itself. She had read of the battles, read of casualties, but that had never brought home to her the awful reality of the war. A people once united, now prepared to kill each other without a second thought. A people brought to this because a wealthy minority, who professed to be God-fearing Christians, objected to the ending of a system which had let them grow rich on the backs and sufferings of others.

The sounds of cannon weren't far away now. Mosa could make out men and horses fighting and falling. She went left to go around the battle but soon came upon a river too deep to cross. She would have to wait until nightfall and then try and slip through the lines.

Come dark, Mosa made her way forward. A full moon lit her path and gave shape to form and shadow. The encampments came right down to the water's edge.

Candlelight shone in the first tent she had to pass. Like some gruesome puppet show behind a see-through curtain a man, saw in hand, stood above another lying on a table. Two others held him down. The screams of the patient made Mosa unsteady. She put out her hand seeking support and touched a pile of what she had thought was wood. A swarm of flies flew up at her. She looked down. Her hand was resting on amputated arms and legs. Maggots squirmed in the exposed flesh. The stench was overwhelming and she retched.

"Who goes there?"

A soldier had appeared, blocking her path.

"Don't shoot," she pleaded as he pointed his rifle at her.

"What in God's name are you doing here?"

"I'm trying to go South to get home."

"You can't cross here. You'll be shot. Go back. Go back the way you came."

Mosa complied and retraced her steps until she was out of his sight. Then she tried again. She inched forward past sleeping soldiers, who were lying out and holding their guns close as though cuddling their loved ones in their dreams. Silently, she navigated her way past the Union forces and into no man's land.

Every one of her limbs trembled. Mosa had crossed the point of no return. If she went back, they would think her the enemy. Go forward and be seen and the Confederates would conclude likewise. But she couldn't stay here. She was out in the open, unprotected like a deer in a meadow.

A shot rang out. Mosa threw herself onto the ground and waited for another. It didn't come. Perhaps it hadn't been aimed at her. Taking no chances, she advanced on her stomach, all the while hugging the edge of the river.

Looking ahead, Mosa saw trees. Raising herself to her knees, she crawled forward. She could hear men's voices to her right, softly talking as their comrades slept. They spoke in that Southern manner, a sound which she had rarely heard since reaching New York. Mosa smiled, she had crossed the line.

She moved on. As the sky lightened to bring another day of death and life-changing injury for the soldiers now behind her, Mosa rested her back against a tree trunk and slept.

The warmth of the sun's rays woke her. She bent over by the river bank, washing the dirt off her hands and face, and then attempted to get the worst of it off her dress.

Hearing movement, Mosa turned her head to see three young black men. They didn't look any older than sixteen. Their clothes were rags, their feet bare.

"Where are you boys going?"

"North to join the Union army," said one.

"You can't get through this way. There's a battle raging up ahead. You'll need to go back until you can cross the river and go up the other side."

"Is that where you're heading ma'am? There's a bridge a mile or two back."

"No, I'm on my way to South Carolina."

"What do you wanna go there for?"

"I've got business there. Do you know where we are?"

"Not far from Richmond, Virginia."

"Thank you, and good luck in getting North."

Their sense of geography proved to be lacking. It took Mosa two long days to reach Richmond. She needed to rest and wash, but the hotels wouldn't accept her. Finally, she found a family willing to give her a room for the night to make some money. Next day, she caught a train heading South. On the first leg of her journey, she had to use the same car as slaves, though car it wasn't, just a boxcar. It brought back unpleasant memories of her journey to Macon.

Mosa pulled her head wrap further down over her face to make sure that her former runaway status was wholly obscured and clutched her bag tightly. It contained her precious papers confirming that she was a free woman. Without them, she would be enslaved again with no brother to come and rescue her this time.

In the boxcar with her were three men, two women, and four children. They were chained together.

"Did you get caught trying to get North?" asked Mosa.

"No," answered one of the women. "We ain't never been in the South before. We was all born and raised free, living peacefully in southern Pennsylvania minding our own business. Then a few weeks back the Confederates attacked. We found ourselves trapped behind their line. We were captured. They say they're taking us South, and we're their slaves now to make up for the ones they lost when they fled North."

Mosa reached out and touched her hand.

"I'm so sorry. Don't lose hope. I truly believe the North will win, and that you'll be free again."

She didn't voice her doubts that it all depended on politics and turned on a dime. Many in the North were tired of war. They would be willing to settle with the South, even let them keep slavery if only they would agree to rejoin the Union. If the Democrats won next year's Presidential election that would be the likely result.

Mosa was let out at stops to stretch her legs. Her fellow passengers weren't. She used the time to buy extra food to share with them.

After various changes of train and more time than she cared to remember, Mosa reached Columbia in South Carolina. There she found a man who would hire out his slave to take her to the plantation on his horse and cart.

For the first time since leaving New York, she began to relax. Only a few miles to go. Mosa congratulated herself. She had survived. She had made it back.

These past few weeks Mosa had seen enough horrors to last her a lifetime; the attack on the orphanage, the cadavers and discarded limbs, the sights and sounds of battle, and the people kidnapped from the North. The plantation would seem like a haven, an island of sanity in this sea of madness. A place where she and those she had come to help could be left in peace to wait out the fighting.

Mosa sat up front with the driver. Closing her eyes, she inhaled the familiar smell of jasmine, the perfume of a South Carolina summer and an antidote to all that she had recently experienced.

"Whoa!"

Her driver had stopped in front of two bedraggled,

white men. They looked malnourished. Both were armed.

"Give us the horse."

"He ain't mine to give, sir. He belongs to my Mas'r."

"Untie him or we'll shoot you and do it ourselves."

The driver jumped down from the cart and did as they asked. One of them swung at his head with the butt of his rifle, knocking the man to the ground.

"That's for making us ask twice."

The two men clambered on the horse and trotted off. The driver got up, rubbing the side of his face.

"Are you all right?" asked Mosa.

"Yeah. I'll walk you to the plantation."

"There's no need. It's only a mile or two from here and you gotta walk back to town."

"I'm taking you. It's not safe round here no more, especially for a lady. Some people would rather shoot you than look at you. We were lucky just now. There's a lot of deserters around making their way home. Their hearts are full of hatred for us. I'll walk back to town at night. I'll be less likely to come across someone in the dark."

CHAPTER 30

As they crested a hill, Mosa saw the plantation laid out below them. She could see workers in the fields harvesting the cotton, the slave quarters, the stables where she had learned to read, and the house where she had once worked. It almost looked idyllic until she reminded herself what it represented.

A dark cloud of sadness passed through her as she remembered Thomas wouldn't be there to greet her. She hoped that he was looking down at her, pleased that she had returned.

"Mosa?" said Jeremiah as he opened the front door in response to her knock. "How'd you get here? You won't have heard about poor Mas'r Thomas."

"I did."

"We all just stayed here, kept working. Waiting for the new Mas'r, whoever he's gonna be."

"You be looking at her now."

"Aw, stop messing with me. That ain't even funny."

"I ain't messing with you, Jeremiah. Thomas left this place to me. The lawyers will be out here the day after tomorrow with the final papers I need to sign."

Jeremiah could see from the look on her face that she was serious.

"Well, as I live and breathe. Never thought I'd see the place belong to a nig-" Jeremiah stopped himself, realizing that he was talking to his new mistress.

"A nigger?"

"Don't mean no disrespect, ma'am."

"It's OK. I've had exactly the same thoughts." It was still surreal to Mosa that she should be back at Old Oaks, and as owner. When she had been forced to lived here she had dreamed of freedom and getting away, never had she thought that she would inherit the plantation. "Can you get Solomon who brought me here from Columbia fed with a decent meal. I need to go wash. I'll be using Thomas' old room. And call everyone in from the fields. I want to speak to them."

Word of who the new mistress was had already spread when Mosa came out of the front door and onto the veranda. She had taken off the dour black dress which she had arrived in, and was now wearing a teal colored one in the latest fashion that she had bought in New York. As she stood there all eyes upon her, Mosa's clothes made a statement. A woman once like them now elegantly dressed. A woman who had found success. She thought it might give them hope that escape from slavery and poverty would soon be a possibility.

"Hi, I'll stay up here so you can all see me as I ain't very tall. I expect it must have come as a surprise to see me come back."

A murmur of agreement went through the assembled number.

"Well, as y'all probably heard by now, Thomas left me the plantation."

"You're one lucky nigger," shouted one of them.

"I sure am," laughed Mosa. "It is my intention to be good to you as I'm sure Thomas was."

"He sure was," said another.

"I'd set you all free if I could, but you must know the law of South Carolina prohibits that. Still, I believe freedom is coming. President Lincoln, God willing, will prevail, and you will all be free. Maybe not this year, but soon. We just gotta find a way to keep going meanwhile.

"Until that time arrives, and after if you want to, I hope you'll stay here and keep working with me. Those of you who want to leave are free to do so. I won't be sending nobody to bring you back. But be careful, it's dangerous out there. I've seen a lot of terrible things on my journey here. The white folk are mad, and happy to take it out on us whenever they get the chance. If you're thinking of joining the Union army, you should be aware if you aren't already, that if you get captured by the Confederates, they won't treat you as prisoners of war but as insurrectionists, and they will hang you."

"And the North is no paradise either. I lived in New York. There's plenty of folks up there afraid once we're free, we'll take their jobs. They'll kill us rather than let us do that.

"I can't predict the future, but right now I believe you're safest staying here. We just need to keep our heads down until it's all over. Then we can reassess the situation.

"I can't pay you. The plantation hasn't been able to sell its cotton for a couple of years. All I can offer is half of any profit I make if we ever get to sell it."

"Why only half?" shouted one of the men. "There's over forty of us and just one of you."

"I want to have enough money to reinvest to keep this place going for those who want to stay living and working here."

"It's easy for you," he shouted back. "A big shot from New York. You ain't suffered like us."

"That's where you're mistaken." Mosa slowly unwound her head wrap. "See this. They branded me for trying to escape when I was sold to a plantation in Georgia. We've all suffered, each and every one of us. But bearing grudges won't feed us. It's time for us to take control of our own destiny. Don't wait on nobody coming to help you, because they won't."

There was no more heckling.

"And I can offer you and your children something of real value, starting from tomorrow. I was fortunate enough to be taught by Thomas to read and write, and I can do some math. In New York, I worked as a teacher in the colored orphanage until it was burned down by jealous white folk. Once freedom comes, those with an education will have an advantage.

"I'll be teaching in the house. The children can come during the day, and those of you adults who wish to learn I can teach in the evenings."

"God bless you, ma'am," called one of the women.

"Yes, God bless you," added others.

"And one last thing. I ain't no ma'am. Just plain old Mosa. I'll let you get to your dinners now. Class for the children begins tomorrow when you head to the fields."

Amongst the crowd, Maisie wiped a tear from her eye, thinking of how this confident, accomplished woman standing before them was the baby who she had saved all those years ago. Now that baby had come back to help them.

"You gone dun us proud, Mosa," said Chloe as she accompanied her back into the house. "Who'd have thought my little helper would become all that you have."

"I've been lucky. I got a break which the rest of you never did. You've all been denied the opportunities everybody should be given. Chloe, how did Thomas die?"

"It were sad, real sad. His daddy took on an overseer, a spiteful man. O'Connell was his name. Thomas fired him shortly after he took over. One night, O'Connell and some others came up here drunk and seeking trouble. Called him a nigger lover and shot him as Thomas sat on his horse, shot him dead."

Mosa put her hand over her mouth to stifle a cry.

"We buried him in the family plot. The men made

him a coffin. They couldn't make a tombstone as none of us knew how to write. We put up a little wooden cross instead."

Walking into Thomas' empty room that evening brought back his loss like a slap to the face. She opened the cupboard and smelled his clothes, seeking some trace of him that still lived. Mosa smiled through her tears when she noticed the letters which she had written him neatly stacked on the nightstand.

But beyond the coziness of the candlelight, the shadows were mournful. When she got into bed and blew out the candle, those shadows seeped into her. Transforming themselves into heavy footed doubts, they ran around her mind, questioning her ability to run the plantation. What if she failed and let everyone down? The confidence which she had to show to others was often little more than a mask, hiding her fear, her fear of failure. She curled up and pulled the sheet over her head for comfort.

CHAPTER 31

Come dawn, Mosa crept out of the house. It was already hot but the humidity hadn't yet begun to climb to the uncomfortable level it soon would when her clothes would cling to her and her forehead would be sticky and covered with droplets of perspiration.

She picked some flowers from the garden and went to the graveyard. On her knees, she carefully laid the flowers under the cross and spoke to the heavens.

"I'm gonna make you proud of me, Thomas. I promise."

As she turned to leave, she noticed a small child of three or four years old watching her from a distance. His eyes were screwed up tightly as if the morning light was too bright for him.

"Hi, who are you?" She smiled at him but he turned and ran.

Not long after Mosa had returned to the house, she heard chatter outside. She opened the front door. At the bottom of the stairs stood a group of excited young children, their faces beaming with delight. Seeing her, they ceased talking and stood there, holding back, still not quite sure if they should walk up onto the veranda and inside. They had never been in the big house before.

"It's OK. You can come up these steps and through this door. No one's gonna bite you. This is your school now."

They whispered to each other and giggled, but as she led them into the lounge they became silent again. Unsmiling portraits of the Elwood family hung on the walls, although there wasn't one of Thomas. Doubtless after Jefferson's killing, their father had decided he would remove the picture of his other son, and Thomas, being a modest man, would have had no wish once he had taken over the plantation for his face to stare down at visitors.

Mosa observed the children cower as they looked up at the paintings as if they feared such people could return at any moment and beat them severely for being here. She decided to get the pictures removed after class. Mosa had no wish to teach under the gaze of slave owners who would have had her whipped for trying to educate these children.

"Now boys and girls, I want y'all to sit cross-legged on the floor."

They instantly did as she commanded. Like puppies waiting to be fed, they sat there looking up at her with hope and wonder.

"I saw a little boy this morning. He had blond hair in tight curls and pale skin. I don't see him here."

The children looked at each other as though checking what, if anything, they should say. They remained quiet.

"I think you know something that you're not telling me. Annie, who is he?"

Annie looked down at the floor.

"Annie, answer me."

"His name's Isaac, Miss," she mumbled. "They tell us not to play with him."

"Who does?"

"The grown-ups. They say he's got the devil in him."

Come evening, the adults arrived. They too happily settled themselves on the floor. Mosa noticed that Maisie's son, Joshua, hadn't come. When class finished, Mosa asked Maisie if she could stay for a moment.

"Is Joshua busy?"

"No, he wouldn't come. Said he'll never be able to learn."

"That's a real shame. Maisie, I never got the chance to thank you, thank you for saving me all those years ago. Thomas told me what you did. It was such a brave thing to do. I owe my life to you."

"It was the right thing to do. And you're more than repaying us all right now."

"I'm trying. There's something I wanted to ask you. I want to know about Isaac, the little albino boy."

"Folk are frightened of him, think he has the evil spirit."

"Do you?"

"I dunno."

"Which means you probably do. Who's his mother?"

"She ran away. Left him behind."

"Who looks after him then?"

"No one in particular. He lives in her hut and gets food that's left over."

"I want to see him in class tomorrow."

Next morning, Isaac came. He sat down apart from the others, shy and silent.

"Children, whatever you may have been told about Isaac here, it isn't true. He's the same as you and me. God just gave him different coloring, like he made you black and white folk white, and me brown. We're all God's children, and we must treat each other with the same kindness and respect. I want you to be nice to him. Don't take no notice of what anybody else says about him."

Mosa wondered if her words would have the desired effect. After class, she took Isaac to the kitchen and fed him. He had hardly uttered a word during the lesson and didn't now. Whenever Mosa got close, he leaned away from her. She realized that she would need to take things slowly with him. He didn't appear to trust anyone, which she considered hardly surprising given that his mother had abandoned him. Mosa had never forgotten how she felt as a child, how she envied the children with mothers to hug them and tell them how much they were loved, and the emptiness in her soul that came from being unwanted and un-cherished.

When she asked Isaac if he'd had enough to eat, he simply nodded and when she said he could go, he ran off as if pleased to escape from her.

Mosa sighed and went out to the fields. Seeing Joshua drinking some water under the shade of an old tree to shelter from the midday sun, she went over to him.

"Hi, Joshua. I was sorry you didn't come to class last night."

"It ain't for me. I was born ignorant and will die ignorant."

"We all were born ignorant, but those who choose to remain so will get left behind in the new world that's coming."

"I'd never manage to learn that stuff. Folk would just make fun of me."

"No one does that in my classes. They're all learn-ing too. We help each other."

"Hmm." His grunt was non committal.

"I've been meaning to thank you for all you've done here since Thomas died. Chloe told me you took the lead and got everyone motivated. Got them to start picking the crop when it was ready."

"Well, there weren't no point letting it rot. Espe-cially after all the hard work we'd done growing it in the first place."

"I was thinking I should put you in charge, but I worry that if the others get educated and you don't, they might not respect you. Could you think seriously about coming to class tonight?"

Joshua laughed. It was a deep and infectious laugh. "I don't know if you're smart, or just plain calculating. OK, I'll be there."

"Thank you. I need someone reliable like you to run this place."

They stored the cotton that they picked that summer in the barn. There was no one they could sell it to. The Union blockade was getting tighter, and the economy of the State continued its downward spiral.

Mosa worried what would happen when the little money which she had left from her inheritance ran out. At least here on the plantation, they grew most of their food. They were fortunate to live on the land at a time like this. Many of those in the towns who relied on buying food were finding it too expensive to afford as a shortage drove up prices.

She unlocked the rifles from the cabinet in the house and gave them to Joshua along with the ammunition which she could find for him to distribute as he saw fit. Many hungry people were roaming the South. People who were desperate enough to kill to survive. Mosa wished she could give food to those who passed by, their bodies gaunt from hunger, but she barely had enough to get those who lived on the plantation through the coming winter.

Each afternoon, she worked her way through the paperwork piled on the desk which Thomas had sat at only a few weeks ago. Much of it was bills. Anxiously, she added them up. There would be little left over, but if her math was correct there was just sufficient.

She came across one envelope addressed to herself. Probably a letter Thomas was going to send her but never did. It had no address, only her name. Mosa tore it open.

My dear Mosa,

If you're reading this, it will be because I am dead and you are here at the plantation.

I'm glad you didn't sell it. I'm sure you'll run it well and to benefit those who live here and depend on this place. When I told you of our family history, there was a part I omitted. I felt you had enough to deal with just finding out about where you came from. But now I am gone, I need your help to look after someone who needs our protection. Our mother.

I hope you won't resent me for not telling you sooner, but it is a sad tale. You see our father, believing she had wronged him by giving birth to you, took her away and had her placed in an asylum in Savannah.

I only found out by chance going through his papers after Maisie told me about you. That's why I disappeared the day when I was supposed to come and take you North. I went to see her.

Unfortunately, she had become mentally deranged. I arranged for her to be moved to Charleston to more sanitary and comfortable accommodation. I have visited from time to time to check upon her well being. Her mental state remains unchanged.

You will receive regular bills for her care under the name of Ethel Smith. The name which our father used for her when he hid her away.

I would ask you to continue to pay them so that she is not thrown into some awful institution.

I am sorry, dear sister, to cause you yet more distress.

Your ever loving brother

Mosa sat back in the chair. The mother who she had never met, never thought she would meet, was still alive.

CHAPTER 32

"If anyone asks, Jeremiah, I have to go to Charleston on business. I'll be back in a few days."

"Shall I get someone to drive you? You shouldn't go alone."

"No, thank you. That won't be necessary."

Down at the stables, she hitched Shadow to the cart. When Mosa neared the city, she slept in the cart. It would be hard for her to find anyone willing to sell her a room for the night, and it would cost money she needed to preserve.

Next morning, she found the house which she wanted. It looked like any other comfortable townhouse where wealthy white folk got to live. Mosa doubted the neighbors would know about the person who lived inside and who almost certainly was never let out. Mosa stood before the green door, her emotions as confused as waters going in different directions and colliding on rapids. She was about to meet someone who meant so little to her, yet should have meant so much, someone who had given her life and should have loved her unconditionally, someone who should have been that incredible person that mothers are.

When the cart rolled back onto the plantation, those old enough to remember stood open-
mouthed. It was as if they were witnessing someone who had arisen from the dead sitting right
by Mosa's side. Although Jane Elwood had aged
considerably, she remained instantly recogniz-
able to them. Some of those watching crossed
themselves, perhaps imploring the Holy Spirit to
protect them against whatever bad fortune this
reminder of the past might bring. Even though she
slowly surveyed those observing her, Jane showed
no emotion or recognition of anyone or anything
as Mosa helped her down and into the house. Her
gaze was fixed and impassive, revealing nothing of
what she might be thinking.

"Jeremiah, we're gonna need Mrs. Elwood's old
room to be made ready. Can you get that taken
care of while I take her to the kitchen to feed her,"
said Mosa as she took Jane's arm and steered her in
the direction she wanted to go.

Chloe dropped the plate which she was holding
when she saw her old mistress. It shattered on the
floor.

"It's OK, Chloe. She's nothing to be afraid of. She
was being looked after in Charleston. There wasn't
enough money left to keep her there so I brought
her back to take care of her."

"Whatever possessed you to do that?"

"It's what Thomas would have wanted."

Chloe shook her head and rolled her eyes to indicate her disapproval.

Mrs. Elwood ate without speaking. She hadn't spoken a single word since the moment Mosa had collected her. If afterward when Mosa led her up the stairs, Mosa had hoped the woman might have given an indication that she knew who her daughter was or where she was on entering her old bedroom, she would have been disappointed. There was none. Her expression remained as blank as it had been since the moment Mosa had first set eyes on her.

"You must be very tired after the long journey. Let's get you ready for bed."

As Mosa pulled back the sheets and sat her down on the bed, Jane Elwood gently put her hand on Mosa's cheek and touched her scar, moving her index finger around it. She looked straight at Mosa as she did so. Tears welled in the eyes of the former mistress of the plantation as she let her hand drop. Her reaction gave Mosa hope, hope that they might find a way to communicate.

"Lay down now. You're safe here. I'll be back in the morning."

Mosa locked the door behind her, debating whether she should at some point mention the name Thomas to Jane to see if it produced any reaction. Mosa decided not to, at least for the time being. Mosa fretted that if she ever did, Jane might want to see him and then be further traumatized that she never could.

With Mosa's mind so focused on her mother, she

had forgotten about the other person depending on her until his absence the following morning reminded her.

"Where's Isaac?" Mosa asked the children in class. Her answer was a wall of silence. "Well?"

"We ain't seen him," volunteered a boy. "Not since the day before yesterday."

After class, Mosa went over to the huts calling out his name repeatedly, but there was no response. Inside the one where Isaac slept, she found only a soiled blanket lying on straw. A growing panic tightened itself around her.

Fists clenched with tension, Mosa hurried back to the house to fetch one of the dogs. She allowed the hound to sniff around inside the hut to absorb Isaac's scent and then let him lead her as he pulled on his leash, nose to the ground and tail wagging as if there was nothing to be concerned about. At a spot amongst trees, the dog began clawing at the earth. Mosa called him off.

Kneeling down, she tore at the soil with her bare hands as though her very life depended on it. There in a shallow grave, he lay. His body had been mutilated.

Mosa emitted a wail of despair. If only she had taken him in and let him live in the house. Isaac had been an outcast, exactly like she had been as a child. His only crime was being different, different to the norm. She had failed to protect him, the one person here who needed her protection more than anyone.

It wasn't many minutes until her sadness turned to rage. She marched around the grounds shouting for Joshua. He appeared from the stables.

"Get everyone here. Now!"

"What for?"

"Just do as I ask," she demanded.

Her chest was still rising and falling noticeably as they came in from the fields, many looking in every direction except hers.

"I want to know who killed Isaac." No one spoke. "You all had a hand in it, did you? Murdering a defenseless little boy, just because he wasn't the same as you. You're no better than the slave owners, condemning people because of their color." Mosa had assumed they were all complicit and saw no need to try and discover the truth. "You and you," she said pointing at two of the men. "You'll dig him a decent grave here on the lawn. And you two, yes you two over there, make him a coffin. And this evening when you get back from the fields, you'll all attend his funeral and pray that God might forgive your wickedness."

It was a somber crowd that gathered as the sun was setting. Mosa didn't acknowledge them when she came off the veranda and walked toward them. They pulled back as if concerned that she would strike one of them. From her expression, it was clear that her fury hadn't abated.

She spoke a few words looking up toward the sky. Her speech was fluent as if she had rehearsed.

"Dear Lord, please accept this innocent child into

heaven and give him eternal peace. Teach us to love everyone regardless of what they may look like on the outside, and forgive all of us for failing Isaac when he needed us most."

She laid down some flowers she carried in her hands and went straight back into the house.

The next morning when the children turned up outside, Chloe appeared at the front door to tell them there would be no class. Mosa remained in the house all day long. And the next day. In the evening, Joshua came over.

"She's sitting out back," said Chloe. "Ain't uttered a single word these past two days."

"Hey," said Joshua, finding her staring into the distance. Mosa turned. She looked drained of emotion and as if she probably hadn't slept since the little boy's death. "I know it was a terrible thing what happened, but you have to understand those involved know no better. When you're told as a child some people are different, bring bad luck, you believe it, even when you're grown. Like white kids are taught that we're barely human and dangerous. Only education can alter the way people think, whatever their color. I understand you being mad, being hurt and all. But don't give up on them. Nothing's gonna change if you just ignore everybody."

Mosa bit her lip and moved her hand across her eyes before looking away to hide her grief.

"I'll go now. Try and get some sleep. You mustn't blame yourself. It wasn't your fault."

The following day, Chloe came down to the quarters to tell the children school was re-opening. It was another week until evening classes for the adults resumed.

Mosa wrote a couple more times to Lloyd, but still there was no response. She knew the army was proficient at delivering letters to soldiers. Correspondence even got through to those taken prisoner. She reconciled herself to the fact that he must surely be dead after so long without sending her a single letter.

Mosa kept her mother fed and clean. Each day she combed Jane's long, unruly hair and put it up to keep her cooler. She doubted that her mother had ever had to do it for herself, even before she had become incapable. All her life she would have been waited upon by slaves, never having to lift a finger except to ring a bell to call for service. The lives of mother and daughter couldn't have been more different. Other than blood, they had nothing in common.

When Mosa had the time to spare she would take her mother on walks outside. Mosa thought something in the house or the grounds would light a candle in Jane's mind but the woman never displayed any emotion as she had that first night. Mosa never mentioned Thomas. What good could come of it? The son who Jane had seen only a handful of times since he was five years old and most likely not knowing that it was him when had gone to visit her, probably not even remembering that she had a child who, unlike Mosa, she had loved.

Mosa took care of her mother out of a sense of duty to Thomas. To Mosa, this wild-eyed person would always remain a stranger. She felt sympathy for Jane that her husband had disowned her and had her locked up in an asylum, but Mosa felt no bond or affection toward the woman, no notion of if only. Even had her mother had a choice in the matter, Mosa knew that she wouldn't have chosen to keep her. At best, she would have had Mosa placed in the slave quarters, or sent elsewhere. At worst, she would have been left out to die. What did Mosa have to thank her mother for?

Winter came and went yet still the war ground on. News didn't often reach them out here. When other plantation owners got together to discuss matters of common interest, Mosa wasn't invited. Gregory Brown rode over one day, the hooves of his horse resounding off a ground hardened by a prolonged dry spell. Mosa was sitting on the rocking chair on the veranda, taking a short but welcome break after morning school before checking with Joshua for any issues arising on the plantation that day. She would then have to deal with paperwork before holding her evening class for the adults. Finally, after dealing with any needs her mother might have, she would retire gratefully to bed for a few hours of sleep.

"Mind if I join you up there?" said her former owner, a man who had never previously given her the time of day.

"No."

He strode confidently onto the veranda as if he owned it.

"What brings you here?"

"Just dropping by."

He sat down heavily in the chair next to hers spreading his legs wide in a display of dominance, giving her a smile which she didn't consider genuine. A shudder ran down her spine. Even after all these years the man's presence made her anxious, despite no longer being his property. She knew Brown must surely want something. At least she now had the freedom to refuse him, unlike the many slave women on whom he had forced himself.

"Never did I think one of my former slave gals would end up with this place. Thomas Elwood leaving it to you is still the talk of the county. There's many think it should be taken off you, not that I'm one of them. How are you finding it, running a plantation?"

"Pretty tough."

"That ain't surprising. You were never brought up to do this. Even a white woman would be likely to fail. I'd be willing to buy it off you for a good price."

Mosa didn't hesitate before she replied.

"Thank you but it's not for sale."

"I'd think carefully about my offer if I were you. Land values are falling all the time. Wait too long and you might not get enough to pay off any debts which you have. And if the Confederacy win, there's no telling what new laws they might pass about free colored folk holding property. Maybe they'll even revoke your freedom. It's not safe for you here. If I were in your shoes, I'd sell the plantation and get back up North while I still could."

"As I said, Mr. Brown, it's not for sale."

He stood up to go, visibly irritated that she should dare to reject his offer.

"If you ever change your mind, you know where to find me. You may have gotten an education, be a teacher and all, but don't assume that makes you educated in the affairs of business. You're missing a golden opportunity."

Climbing back on his horse, he pulled hard on the reins, swinging the creature around before galloping away.

Mosa was hot with anger. How dare he assume a woman, especially a woman who wasn't white, couldn't make a go of it. His condescension only strengthened her determination to succeed. Exhausted she may be but she wasn't going to give up.

Her teaching alone had already achieved much. Mosa derived a deep satisfaction from seeing her students reading. She had made the bookshelves in the house a library for all. Anyone was welcome to come and borrow whichever book they liked. She had even seen Joshua sneak in there and take one.

Mosa relied heavily on him. They spoke together

almost every day and became good friends. She considered that they now knew each other well enough for her to mention what others had already told her.

"I was sorry to hear about your wife," she said as they sat on the ground by the side of the stables one spring evening as birds dived for bugs in the air above them.

"It was hard. And the baby died the day after she did."

"How long ago is it now?"

"A couple of years."

"Weren't you tempted to run? Go North and start a new life."

"I was but my brothers beat me to it. With Pa gone, I had to stay and be here for Mama."

"Did you never think about remarrying?"

"Not really. What can I offer? I own nothing. And I always feared being broken apart, being sold away from one another at any time. I've had enough hurt already without setting myself up for more."

"You're too hard on yourself, Joshua. You have a lot to offer. And you can read and write now. You could do well when this war is over."

"Thanks to you."

"Thanks to both of us. I couldn't keep this place going on my own, not without you."

"And you. Don't you ever wish you would have married?"

"I did once but I've twice been disappointed. Not that it was the fault of either of them. Circumstances got in the way. Just wasn't meant to be, I guess. There's no point worrying about something you can't change. It eats away at you if you let it. We need to focus on those things we can control, those things where we can make a difference. And you have made a difference. To me and everyone else living here. You're a good man, Joshua."

Without thinking she placed her hand on his, withdrawing it almost immediately after she had done so, embarrassed by her forwardness.

"You didn't need to do that," he said looking at her with his large brown eyes and his dark skin shining in the glow of the sinking sun.

"I'm sorry, I wasn't thinking."

"That's not what I meant. You didn't need to take your hand away."

Mosa stood up quickly, patting down her dress as if she needed to demonstrate that her hands were occupied and not meant for him.

"I really must get back to the house. I have so much still to do before bed."

CHAPTER 33

As 1864 unfolded further, reports began to filter through that Union soldiers under the command of General William Tecumseh Sherman had marched into Georgia. They lived off the land, taking whatever they needed, and burning plantations as they went. In September Atlanta fell, propelling Lincoln to re-election in November.

Many liberated slaves joined the back of Sherman's convoy, but he made no allowances for them. At one river to halt his pursuers, he ordered the destruction of the pontoon which his men had constructed as soon as they had crossed it. That was before the former slaves could reach the bridge, leaving them to the vengeance of the enraged Confederates.

Sherman's men, nicknamed the Little Devils, took Savannah before Christmas and then swung north toward South Carolina. Even in the coastal swamps, they advanced at over ten miles a day, carrying their rifles above their heads.

When one late January morning in 1865 Mosa found her mother dead in bed, she shed no tears. Mosa done what Thomas had wanted. Now that obligation was satisfied.

There was no real funeral to speak of. While Mosa recited a short prayer, the men finally buried Jane in the place everyone had thought, until recently, that she had been laid to rest many years earlier.

Although neither of her parents had wanted her, Mosa wasn't bitter. Mosa considered herself extremely fortunate. She'd had a brother who had looked out for her. Many of those living on the margins never found anyone to care about them, like poor little Isaac. She would always regret not saving him. Like a rock in her stomach, Mosa carried a guilt inside her for failing the boy, a guilt which she felt sure would accompany her to the grave.

In February, Joshua took a horse and cart to Columbia to purchase some supplies. He returned empty-handed.

"What happened?" asked Mosa.

"The town's being burned to the ground. Some folk say the Confederates caused it, leaving cotton bales burning in the street, others that it was Sherman's men. Either way, the place is aflame like the end of the world has come. Those Union soldiers are gonna be heading this way mighty soon. They're razing everything to the ground as they go. One man told me Sherman hates South Carolina most of all. He says it's where treason began and where it will end."

"I must go talk to them. When I tell them this plantation is owned by me, a former slave, they'll leave us alone."

"I'll come with you."

"No need, they're already here."

Coming down the hill, they observed a line of soldiers.

"I'm going out to meet them."

Joshua grabbed her arm.

"Mosa, stop. What color uniform do you see? They ain't Union soldiers, they're Confederates."

"Will you get the rifles?"

"We've only four of them. We couldn't stop them, there's too many, and they'd probably kill all of you in revenge if we tried. Maybe they'll just want some food and then be on their way."

Mosa, Joshua, and the others stood watching, hoping that these harbingers of death might pass on by and leave them alone. They didn't. Inexorably, the band of men kept marching toward them as if ants which refused to be diverted from their goal and which would devour all in their path.

It was only minutes until they arrived. Unshaven, their uniforms covered in grime and smelling of stale sweat, there were about thirty of them in total.

"Who's in charge round here?" demanded a man with unwashed auburn hair and eyes which were bitter and unforgiving.

"I am the owner of this plantation," said Mosa stepping forward. "I'm a free woman."

"Well, well. Fellas, this is the nigger owned plantation folk have been talking about. A vision of the future, where property is owned by Negroes and the white man is made homeless in his own land if we don't stop those damn Yankees. I worked here once as overseer. The owner was a nigger lover. He fired me because I called him out for what he was. Let them run the place, he did. They did whatever they wanted, just like now it would seem."

Mosa swallowed hard. The man in front of her was O'Connell. Her brother's killer stood just feet away from her, unrepentant and never to be held accountable for his crime.

"Bring us some food and drink," he commanded.

Mosa nodded at Chloe and together they went into the house, returning with ham, cornbread, and a bottles of bourbon. O'Connell was unimpressed.

"What's this? Don't go hiding all the food you have. I bet you got a load more than that, living here in luxury while we've been forced to scavenge like animals. Bring out all you got or I'll have you whipped."

Mosa and Chloe fetched all the food they had in the kitchen which could be eaten without needing first to be cooked.

The soldiers ate on the lawn as if they hadn't had a good meal in weeks, consuming what would have lasted those on the plantation for many days.

"I say we stay, ambush the Yankees. They're likely coming right through here if what we know of their plans is correct," said one of the soldiers.

"Good idea," agreed O'Connell. "We can hide in the house."

"What about the slaves?" asked another. "They'll give us away,"

"We'll lock them in the barn over there. And if any of you make any noise, any noise at all when the Yankees come," said O'Connell looking menacingly at Mosa and the others who stood huddled together, "we'll set it on fire with you in it. Right, let's get them in there boys."

Prodding them with their rifles as though they were herding cattle, they forced Mosa and the slaves into the barn and slid the wooden lock across the double doors so that they couldn't be opened from within.

Inside, it was cramped amongst the cotton bales. Mothers whispered to their children, emphasizing the importance of remaining quiet. None of them doubted that these men would carry out their threat. The safety they thought they enjoyed living out here and keeping out of sight had proved to be illusory.

Outside, it had become eerily silent. The Confederates, it appeared, had retreated to the house.

"Joshua, I need your help to get out of here. I've got to go warn the Union soldiers," said Mosa.

"But you might be killed."

"If I don't go, we'll all be killed. Those men ain't never gonna set us free. Once they've shot the Yankees, they'll set this place on fire with us in it. I'm convinced of it."

"I'm coming with you."

"No, I need you to stay. Someone needs to be in

charge and keep everybody calm. Only you can do that."

"OK. There's an opening for ventilation on the side. If you climb on my shoulders, you can squeeze through. Hey y'all," he said calling for attention, "Mosa's going for help. When I cough, I want you to start singing a spiritual to cover the noise of her leaving."

Heads nodded at him in the half-light.

Joshua and Mosa maneuvered their way past the cotton bales until they stood beneath the small opening.

"You take good care of yourself now," said Joshua.

"You too."

How it happened, she couldn't recall. Had she leaned toward him, or he to her, or had they both intuitively moved in together. Their lips met. It was a kiss which had been long in the making, too shy for too long to reveal itself in all the days which they had spent together. They both wanted it to last longer, but they didn't have the gift of time.

Joshua held her face in his hands.

"Stay safe."

"And you."

Joshua bent down so that she could climb onto his shoulders and then he carefully stood. He coughed, calling forth a low and mournful sound from the captive choir.

Mosa pulled herself into the opening, turning herself around as she went through it. She lowered her legs, still gripping with her hands before letting go and falling to the ground with a thud.

"Shut the hell up, or I'll set this place on fire right now," shouted a soldier from outside.

The singing inside came to an abrupt end.

Mosa stood against the barn, her pulse racing. Less than a hundred feet away were trees that would give her cover, however the space in between was visible from the house. She waited, paralyzed with fear. But she had no choice, she had to move. At any moment one of those soldiers could appear. There was no safe place here.

Holding her dress up, she made a run for it, her head down and her shoulders hunched as if that could somehow protect her. There was no shout, no bullet. Reaching the trees, she looked back at the barn. Over forty people in there were depending on her. Mosa's breathing was fast and shallow. The stress of such a responsibility frightened her.

She began walking toward Columbia, following the rutted track and ready to dive into the undergrowth should she see anyone. Her mind tormented her. Would she make it, and if she did would the Union soldiers reach the plantation in time before Joshua, Maisie, and everyone else were burned alive?

As it got dark, the orange glow of a city in flames guided her closer.

"What do you want?" demanded a suspicious voice.

A Union soldier stepped into her path.

"I need to see your captain. I have news about a planned ambush against your men."

The soldier led her toward a group of Union soldiers sitting around a fire, warming themselves against the winter night. He went over to one of them, who stood and came over to Mosa.

"I am the captain."

In the flickering shadows there was something familiar about him, something that reminded her of someone under that beard.

CHAPTER 34

Leaning forward a little, Mosa stared at him intently. Did she know him, or did he just look like a person that she used to know?

"Lloyd?" Her voice was uncertain.

"Mosa?"

"It is you. Thank God you're alive. I was certain you were dead."

"I should be. I've had many close calls. If I were a cat, I think this would be my ninth life. What on earth are you doing here?"

"It's a long story. I've come to warn you and your men. A bunch of Confederate soldiers have taken over our plantation and are hiding in the house. They've locked the slaves in the barn and are going to attack you and your men."

"You are a brave woman, Mosa, risking your life to help us."

"Not really. I was locked in that barn too. I'm sure they intend to burn it down with everyone in it."

"Why did you return here, to a plantation in the South?"

"It's complicated. I'll explain when this is all over."

"Can you lead us there?"

"Gladly."

"Good, we'll attack at dawn. You must be hungry, come with me. I'll get you something to eat."

They sat down on the ground a short distance away from the group of men by the fire.

"I wrote to you so many times, Lloyd. Didn't you get my letters?"

He looked down at the ground, avoiding the penetrating gaze of those eyes which had once bewitched him so.

"I did. I hope you can forgive me for not responding. It...it just seemed easier that way."

"Easier? How?"

"When I was in Washington, I met someone. When you think you may well die the next day, caution is thrown to the wind. She fell pregnant and we got married. I haven't seen her or my son for a couple of years. I was ashamed of what I'd done to you. I thought it best not to reply to your letters, let you believe that I had perished. I'm sorry, Mosa. You deserve better, better than me."

"Oh, Lloyd."

Mosa reached out her hand to his. She didn't feel anger or sorrow. Relief was the emotion she felt, relief that he was alive, accompanied by relief that she was without obligation to him. There was a new song in her heart now.

"It's OK. It really is. War changes us all."

"Thank you for being so understanding. You are a special lady, Mosa. I should go brief my men."

The sky was a carpet of stars with no hint of dawn as they set off. Their breath created tiny clouds in the cold air. Mosa led the way with Lloyd. When they got close, a couple of men stayed back to look after the horses.

As the first rays of sun fell on the hill, they descended into the grounds of the plantation. The soldiers advanced in a broad line through grass wet with morning dew. In peacetime, experiencing daybreak would have raised their spirits but not today. This would be another day of death. None of them felt exhilaration. Instead, they carried a deep unease as though daylight would suffocate them as they inhaled with short, sharp breaths. Despite all the battles which they had survived, they had to fight fear each day, fear that this would be their last day on earth.

The stillness of early morning was broken by gunfire coming from the house. They had been seen. They dropped to the ground and started returning fire, moving forward gradually.

"Look," shouted one of the soldiers.

Mosa turned to her left. The barn had been set alight. The man who had done this ran back toward the house until he was cut down by a Union shot.

Lloyd barked out commands to his men. They fanned out further, around the sides and back of the house until they had it surrounded.

Mosa rushed over to the barn. Massive flames like angry genies released from a lamp escaped skyward, enveloping the front of the building. The door was already inaccessible.

She ran around to the side. A man dropped to the ground out of the opening Mosa had taken yesterday, then another and another. They stood beneath it, catching women and children as they fell down toward the earth. More men then followed until no one else emerged.

"Is everyone out?" asked Mosa anxiously.

"Joshua's still in there. He was helping everyone out. Got them to climb on him. He can't get out."

Mosa ran off toward the stables to fetch the ax. Upon entering, she halted in surprise. A man was already in there, climbing up onto Shadow. It was O'Connell. Seeing her, he went for his pistol. Mosa threw herself behind a bale of straw to avoid the shot.

The gunfire spooked Shadow who neighed loudly and rose up on her hind legs. O'Connell was thrown to the ground. His gun went flying. He lay there motionless, temporarily winded.

Mosa got up and grabbed the ax hanging on the wall. She went over to where he lay.

"This is for killing my brother."

She raised the ax so that she could bring it crashing down on his chest and punish him for what he had done, for the hatred that he had shown not just for Thomas but for everyone here.

They both yelled in horror. Mosa stopped, the ax in mid-air. She couldn't do it. She hadn't succeeded in killing before and wouldn't this time.

O'Connell mocked her weakness.

"Once a slave, always a slave."

She could have killed him, but now she would die. He reached out his arm to grab his gun and raised his upper body preparing to shoot her.

There was an angry snorting noise. Going up on her back legs once more, Shadow landed her front hooves hard on O'Connell, time after time, stamping on him with fury as O'Connell screamed out in pain. Mosa watched, transfixed. It was as if Thomas' horse remembered this man, remembered what he had done. Shadow didn't stop until O'Connell was silent, his face a bloody mess. He was dead.

Ax in hand, Mosa ran from the stable to the barn. In a frenzy, she hacked away at the wood on the back wall until she had made a hole through which she could crawl.

Inside, it was difficult to see. Smoke stung her eyes.

"Joshua. Joshua," she called out in between coughs as she inhaled.

There was no reply.

Mosa saw a body lying face down, lifeless. She made her way toward it on her hands and knees in an attempt to keep beneath the smoke. As she advanced, Mosa glanced frequently upward at the burning roof, terrified it could fall upon them at any moment.

She heaved him onto his back and stood, half bent over. Taking Joshua under the arms, she began pulling him toward the opening she had made.

"Over here," those outside shouted at her.

Mosa shrieked as a burning beam fell, missing them both by inches. She fell to her knees, exhausted and gasping for air. It was no good. Mosa couldn't go any further. She just couldn't. She felt herself losing consciousness as she flopped forward onto the ground next to Joshua.

CHAPTER 35

Concerned faces peered down at her and filled her field of vision.

"She's coming round."

"Praise the Lord."

Mosa wondered where she could be. Her bed was hard. She felt it with her hands. It was unyielding. She raised her head a little and they pulled back. She could see grass, and in the gaps between people the barn, though barn it was no longer. It had become a pyre of burning wood. She thought of only one thing.

"Joshua?"

"Over there."

Mosa pushed herself up with her hands so that she could see. He lay there, not far from her, his head to one side, away from her. She crawled over to him. His clothes, or what was left of them, were black with soot. There were burns on his body and he wasn't moving.

"Joshua, don't leave me. Please. I can't manage without you. Joshua!"

His head turned toward her.

"You don't get rid of me that easy."

"Oh Joshua, you're alive."

Mosa threw herself on him and hugged him with delight.

"Ow woman. That hurts."

"Sorry," she said recoiling quickly. "We're gonna get you better, I promise."

She stood up, taking a nearby helping hand for support. It was Maisie.

"The fighting's over," she said. "But look at the house."

Fire spilled out of the windows like an erupting volcano. Several of the slaves had formed a line to the pond, passing buckets of water along, but their efforts were in vain.

"That white paint work'll be as black as me when it's over," added Maisie.

"What about the soldiers, the Union soldiers?"

"It seems only one of them got shot."

Mosa walked across to where they were creating a mound of corpses, unceremoniously dropping the bodies of the dead Confederates they had carried.

"You should burn them to stop disease spreading," said a Union soldier.

"Where's Captain Jenkins?"

"Right there."

Two men stood in front of him. They moved back as she approached. He lay on his back, his head propped up by a soldier's folded jacket.

"Mosa." His voice cracked as if speaking must be a huge effort for him.

"Lloyd, what happened?"

"I got shot."

"Don't you worry. I'll take care of you."

Lloyd removed his hand from his chest revealing blood, blood which was still flowing out of him.

"I wish you could. Spending time with you would be nice. Can you… can you write to my wife? Tell her…tell her I love her and our little boy."

Tears ran down Mosa's face, collecting soot from her cheeks as they did so and falling like black raindrops on the earth. She got down beside him and held his hands in hers.

"Of course I will. Thank you, Lloyd. Thank you for fighting for us."

"We did it, Mosa. We did it. You and me."

He tried to smile but the corners of his mouth defied him and wouldn't move. The life went out of him, like a tide going out which would never come back in.

She closed his open eyes. Sniffing to maintain her composure, Mosa got up from her knees.

"We'll bury him here in a grave fitting for his sacrifice."

"Appreciate it, ma'am," said one of the soldiers standing near her. "We gotta move out now. At least this goddamn war will soon be over."

As the charred remains of the house smoldered, Mosa had some of the men dig a grave. Others brought a coffin. They all gathered around as it was lowered into the ground. Once again Mosa found herself placing flowers on the soil as someone said a few words commending the soul of

Lloyd Jenkins to God.

Covered in dirt and weary to her core, Mosa wandered away. She was wiping her sore eyes when Maisie approached her.

"How's Joshua doing?" asked Mosa.

"He's suffering. It'll be a while but he'll recover, thanks to you saving him."

"I never thought I'd lose it all."

"I can understand how the house must have meant a lot to you."

"No, it didn't. Really. It meant nothing at all. None who lived there cared about us, except for Thomas. I don't need a big house to be happy. But with the barn destroyed, we've lost all our cotton. I'd planned on selling it as soon as the war ended so I'd have money to keep going and some to share with all of you. There's nothing left. It's all gone, every last bit."

"Freedom was never gonna be easy, Mosa, but it'll be a whole lot better than what went before, money or no money. You should be proud, very proud of what you've done."

"What we've all done, Maisie," said Mosa putting her arm around her. "What we've all done."

ALSO BY DAVID CANFORD

Sweet Bitter Freedom

The sequel to *The Throwback.* Though the Civil

War has ended, Mosa is confronted by new challenges. Her husband becoming a politician seems to offer a new dawn but his election to office has unexpected consequences. With lives in danger, Mosa makes a life-changing decision. Will she and her family ever find real safety and true freedom?

Bound Bayou

A young teacher from England achieves a dream when he gets the chance to work for a year in the United States, but 1950s Mississippi is not the America he has seen on the movie screens at home. When his independent spirit collides with the rules of life in the Deep South, he sets off a chain of events he can't control.

Kurt's War

Kurt is an English evacuee with a difference. His father is a Nazi. As Kurt grows into an adult and is forced to pretend that he is someone he isn't for his own protection, will he survive in the hostile world in which he must live? And with his enemies closing in, will anyone believe who he really is?

A Heart Left Behind

New Yorker, Orla, finds herself trapped in a web of secret love, blackmail and espionage in the build up to WWII. Moving to Berlin in the hope of escaping her past, she is forced to undertake a task that will cost not only her life but also her son's if she fails.

Betrayal in Venice

Sent to Venice on a secret mission against the Nazis, a soldier finds his life unexpectedly altered when he saves a young woman at the end of the Second World War. Many years later, Glen Butler discovers the truth. His reaction betrays the one he loves most, his daughter.

Going Big or Small

A Man Called Ove meets Thelma and Louise. Retiree, Frank, gets more adventure than he bargained for when he sets off across 1980s Europe hoping to shake up his mundane life. Falling in love with a woman and Italy has unexpected consequences.

A Good Nazi?

Growing up in 1930s Germany two boys, one Catholic and one Jewish, become close friends. After Hitler seizes power, their lives are changed forever. When World War 2 comes, will they help each other, or will secrets from their teenage years make them enemies?

When the Water Runs out

Will water shortage result in the USA invading Canada? One person can stop a war if he isn't killed first, but is he a hero or a traitor? When two very different worlds collide, the outcome is on a knife-edge.

2045 The Last Resort

In 2045 those who lost their jobs to robots are taken care of in resorts where life is an endless vacation. For those still in work, the American dream has never been better. But is all quite as perfect as it seems?

SIGN UP

Don't forget to sign up to receive David Canford's email newsletter at DavidCanford.com including information on new releases and promotions and claim your free ebook

ABOUT THE AUTHOR

David started writing stories for his grandmother as a young boy. They usually involved someone being eaten by a monster of the deep, with his grandmother often the hapless victim.

Years later as chair lady of her local Women's Institute, David's account of spending three days on a Greyhound bus crossing the United States from the west coast to the east coast apparently saved the day when the speaker she had booked didn't show up.

David's life got busy after university and he stopped writing until the bug got him again recently.

As an indie author himself, David likes discovering the wealth of great talent which is now so easily accessible. A keen traveler, he can find a book on travel particularly hard to resist.

He enjoys writing about both the past and what might happen to us in the future.

Cambridge University educated, his previous jobs include working as a mover in Canada and a sandblaster in the Rolls Royce aircraft engine factory. David works as a lawyer during the day. He has three daughters and lives on the south coast of England with his wife and their dog.

A lover of both the great outdoors and the man-made world, he is equally happy kayaking, hiking a trail or wandering around a city absorbing its culture.

You can contact him by visiting his website at DavidCanford.com

Made in the USA
Monee, IL
05 July 2021